YOU
MAKE
ME
HAPPY

Acknowledgements

First and foremost, I'd like to thank my family for their unwavering support and encouragement in everything I pursue, even though they didn't know this book was in the works until the day it was published. This book, in a way, is a surprise for them. Maa, Papa, and my dearest little brother, I hope you feel immense happiness and pride when you hold this book in your hands.

It is my pleasure to thank my friend Gunjan for her constant support, for receiving untimely calls, and for brainstorming with me whenever I was in a bind. I am deeply grateful to my friend Nuvorish for his unbiased feedback and corrections. Thank you for being my unpaid editor; we can discuss your cut later, so you don't have to worry.

I must mention some friends who didn't help with the book directly but whose presence in my life is invaluable. They did play cameo roles in this book if that counts as a reason. Thank you for your constant support and encouragement. Shivraj, thank you for planting the seed in my mind that I could actually write something. If it weren't for you, it would have been impossible for me to start this roller coaster of a journey.

My friends Suhel, Tannu and Lokesh made this journey more joyful. I give my sincere thanks to Sagar and Prashant for their technical support—they know what I mean.

Finally, I thank everyone who believed in me. This book stands as much as a physical embodiment of your faith as it does of my dreams. I hope it brings you as much joy in reading it as it has brought me in creating it. Thank you from the bottom of my heart for being a part of this journey.

CHAPTER 01: I AM STUPID!

I am stupid! He thinks. Finds himself standing at the edge of a sky-high rooftop restaurant that he somehow managed to break into. He looks down. Desolate roads wait for the people, people yet to get up and start the hustle. The clear sky coloured in a mix of orange and blue with some hint of clouds looks completely colourless to him, all he can see is the absence of trees in this "industrial" city. Getting hit by continuous blows of wind; he continues to stare at the dim rising sun.

'Am I not scared of heights?' he asks himself.

But that is not what's important at all.

He mutters again, 'Life does turn around in a moment, especially the way you never expect it to. One day you are the happiest man on earth and the next day you are a pathetic loser crying over a breakup. Instead of looking forward and doing something incredible with my life, I ended up being a sore loser still struggling to move on from my first heartbreak. It's been four months;

I still can't move on. What does '*move on*' even mean?'

As usual, his last conversation with her begins to play in his head.

'Listen, Shweta, I am sorry, okay? I don't know what happened to me…'

'You broke up over a text Shivansh! Didn't you owe me an explanation?' Shweta cried.

'I know I was wrong, I can explain…' he tried to speak again.

'Listen, Shivansh. Before you say anything, I want to make it clear that whatever it is that you want to say, I'll hear it out but don't expect us to be together anymore,' she declared and stopped speaking, waiting to hear from him.

Shivansh tried to put together some words to explain everything that had happened. He knew that once she was set on something, no one, not even him, her boyfriend, could change her mind.

When the explanation came to an end, she responded the way she said she would, and Shivansh knew that, but he couldn't bear it.

She just said, 'Okay I get what you went through, but this is not going to work.'

Regardless, He spent hours to make her come back to him. Like any other young boy in love, he trashed his ego and begged her to be with him. He said everything he could, but nothing changed her mind. With this, the phone call ended and with it ended the long-distance relationship of just over eight months. The love he doubted he deserved, the love he saw forever in, was gone.

As the conversation in his mind comes to an end, he starts to feel his surroundings again. The sun stares back at him more intensely, making his eyes hurt. The winds grow stronger. He remembers why he climbed this building at this odd time. A chill goes down his spine, but he strengthens his resolve and decides not to turn back, and jump.

'5…'

'4…'

'3…'

'2…'

He stops. He can't do it. Standing at the edge, ready to jump, he sees his mother's face when his whole life flashes before his eyes. Just the thought of the look on his mother's face, when she hears the news, makes him not only rethink his decision but completely change it. He decides not to jump, willingly this time. He decides to give life a second chance, to do something meaningful with his life, and move on, for his mother.

'I need to get a new job,' he chuckles as he remembers leaving his last job the day before.

He turns around to get down from the parapet, and his foot slips. He tries to move his body to fall on the roof but fails. He starts to fall through the building. He is shocked but it is too late anyway, there's nothing he can do now. He stops thinking. He wants to think about the most important people for him in his last moments. With his body accelerating towards the ground, he feels the fear and regret he never knew.

I could have done better, I don't know if I should have sent that last letter to you, but I wish it finds its way to you, he thinks and keeps his eyes open as long as he can, watching the sky till his last breath.

He jumps out of his bed, screaming. He is drenched with sweat, panting heavily. He runs to the bathroom as he feels vomit rushing above his throat. It feels like life itself is getting drained out of his body, he falls on the wet floor after vomiting his guts out. He feels strange and weak but somehow manages to get up and goes to wash his face. Turns on the lights, too bright. He covers his eyes and slowly tries to look for the tap. As he begins to wash his face, he looks into the mirror and sees something unbelievable. Shocked. Again. He looks young, too young for someone in his twenties. Not even a single sign of facial hair, skinny body, height less than he can remember, everything he sees in himself tells him that he's just a kid.

'No, no, no, this is not happening. This can't be real. This has to be a dream!' he talks to himself. Then he notices that even his voice is different but somehow familiar. It's like when he was younger. He goes back to his bed; it isn't the same either. His younger brother is there, sleeping, free from all the care in the world, in his bed! And to his surprise, he doesn't just look younger, but he is just a child. He looks around the house. Looks at the calendar since he can't find his phone. Everything is pointing to one possibility, that he could have only dreamt of. He is ten years back in time! He remembers he used to live with his parents back in those days so, they must be in the other room. He goes to the other room on his toes and feels so relieved to see his mother's face. She is awake, probably hearing his scream.

'Beta, did you have a bad dream? I heard you scream,' she says in the kindest voice on earth.

'Maybe… I don't remember but I'm fine now. Just came to check if you were awake, and you are, thanks to me, Sorry maa,' he says.

'No worries beta. Did you drink some water?' she asks still worried about his son and not even thinking about her sleep.

'Hanji maa, I just came from the kitchen. You don't have to worry. Now go back to sleep, okay? Good night maa,' he says with a smile.

'Good night beta'

I can't believe I am back in time, about ten years I think, he thinks. *If this is real and I wake up in this same room the next day, then I know what I have to do…*

CHAPTER 02: IT IS REAL

Shivansh cannot sleep. He checks his phone again and again,

02:34 pm...

02:35 pm...

02:38 pm...

02:45 pm...

03:03 pm ...

As usual, the alarm goes off, but Shivansh can't get up. Half asleep Shivansh feels a warm hand gently pulling his cheek.

'Uth jaa mere raja beta,' says his mother. 'It's already 06:30!' she continues. Shivansh struggles to leave his warm blanket.

Seeing Shivansh devouring his breakfast at an unusual speed his mother wonders if everything is alright. 'What happened?' she asks.

'Hmm?' says Shivansh with food stuffed in his mouth, completely oblivious to what his mother is talking about.

'You got ready so quickly and having breakfast right now without turning on the television. It's not a usual sight to see. Everything good?' she finally asks unable to hold any longer.

'Umm Yes maa it's just that the exams are coming...' he can't think of a better excuse. Of course, he is hungry, he's been hungry since he vomited everything out. His mother and father can't hold back any longer and start guffawing.

'Since when did you start worrying about your exams? Anyway, just keep studying in moderation and we're sure you'll do good,' he can't believe what his strict father said. He pats Shivansh's head and begins to leave for work.

'Papa, what's the date today?' Shivansh asks with some hesitation.

'14th August, why?'

'Nothing, just...' he can't ask which year for obvious reasons.

'Beta it's about time, don't you need to leave too? You also woke up late today,' his mother says.

'Hanji Mummy Ji, I am ready and about to leave'

It took him 30 minutes to reach school instead of five. He is somewhat hoping for all that is happening to be real, time travel or whatever it is, he is not 26 anymore, he is 13 and in 8th standard. Impossible to believe but he can't just turn a blind eye to everything that is happening.

He is a bit late and sees everyone heading for the assembly hall. He rushes to reach his class, throws his schoolbag on a bench, and gets back to the assembly hall. Lost in his never-ending thoughts figuring out what to do in this new life, a new opportunity in front of him, and what led to all of this, he can't notice anything that's happening. He is still thinking about his last morning as an adult, *I cannot believe I failed twice yesterday, I went to jump but gave up, then tried to live a life but fell. How is that even possible? How can someone be so unlucky and dumb at the same time? And here I am ten years back in time like nothing ever happened, everyone is behaving the same way I remember them from my past. Did it only happen to me? Why me? I am not a hero or something that has to save the world or anything like that, or am I? I was just sad about not being together with the one I loved. I only cared about her, nothing else. So why did something as grand as this happen to me?* He finds himself sitting in his old class after the assembly is over. He notices some familiar faces; some he had forgotten and some he could never forget. He feels nostalgic to be in his class and all the continuous noise, it was certainly vastly different from a regular reunion.

The bell rings, somewhat suppressing the noise and finally, the noise fades away completely when the teacher enters the classroom. Everyone gets up and wishes Mrs Rekha in harmony, 'Goooood moooorniiiiingg Maaa'aam.'

The class begins. Shivansh still looks around to find the one person he cares about. To his amazement, he sees Shraddha. How can he forget that she would be here too? She was his first crush. He still remembers the way he felt about her, the way she made his insides squirm. There was a time when all he could think about was her. However today, it is completely different, he can't feel anything for her. He knew this would happen but was still somewhat taken aback by how seeing his *first crush* made him feel nothing at all. *I guess that's the difference between a teen and an adult or maybe affection and love...* he wonders.

The lunch time is about to get over and Mrs. Rekha enters the class again, not to take the next class but for an announcement.

'Keep quiet everyone!' she shouts in her sweet voice and continues, 'We have a new friend.'

And there she is. Her innocent puppy eyes only search for a seat, not anyone to talk to or introduce herself. She smiles enough to make others believe that she's not nervous. Her cheeks and ears are as red as a strawberry, but it looks charming over her pearl-white skin. She looks like Snow White but with hazel eyes. She brings this unexplainable aura that fills the class with a sense of comfort. She is holding her bag straps with her tiny hands, the hands that Shivansh loves, they look sensitive like feathers. As soon as she notices an empty seat, she doesn't waste a second to blend in with the class and stop being the centre of attention.

Walking weirdly to the seat, she places her bag on the bench and sits. Shivansh is sitting at the back, he can see her braids. *Damn! She looks so cute even in those 'champu' braids,* he thinks.

She is small, not short but small. Small enough to be easily mistaken as a Pokémon. She's a little chubby too, but Shivansh knew that the last thing on earth she wants to be called is fat.

Her showing up in class spread an unsettling environment, which was normal for kids at their age. Whenever new students arrive, everyone wants to know more about them. Girls surround her and ask her all kinds of questions.

'What's your name?'

'Where are you from? Why did you come mid-semester?'

'What do you like? Do you like Justin Bieber?'

Some even offered her help, 'You can take the notes from me, I'll show you around, if you need any help just ask, don't be shy.' Mrs. Rekha gets angry to see them acting like that, so she raises her voice slightly but enough for the class to notice and makes the girls return to their seats saying, 'During your free time!'

Shivansh is in love, again. Wondering if it is possible to fall in love with the same person all over again. He is looking at her, he cannot think of anything else. Someone says something to him, he only hears a blur murmur, unable to make out who is saying what. Cheerlessly, he shifts his focus from her to Aakash, the one sitting just next to him, his best friend, and says, 'What?'

'Are you crying?' Aakash chuckles.

'No!' replies Shivansh as a reflex and notices big droplets rolling down his cheeks, 'Something's in my eye, eyes, yes both of them' and laughs. Everyone around him laughs to witness this comic scene. He wipes the tears with his handkerchief and acts as if he is trying to get something out of his eyes.

To think that Shweta would arrive on the first day of my new life, what a start! he thinks but his face becomes pale as texts of their break-up conversation begin to float in front of his eyes.

> Break up

> I want to

What happened? Are you good?

> You know the thing we discussed, about time, you were right. I do need more of your time.

Yar I can't do anything about this time situation, we've talked about this

> I know.

You sure?

> Yes.

> You are not joking or anything, right?

> No.

> Okay.

> Sorry for everything.

> Yar please.
> Just stop.

> Okay then.

> Yeah, bye.

{after two hours}

> You sure? This is not a prank or something, is it?

> Yar please, don't make this harder.

> Okay sorry It's still hard to believe, it'll take some time to digest.

He deleted the chat box after her last text. It took over four minutes to completely wipe out 92,874 messages. *I wonder how many texts were from her,* he thought. It was more than thrice the rest of his chat boxes combined. *Is that all it takes to break up?* He thought.

The bell rings again to bring Shivansh back to his new reality. It's a sports class. The whole class is now waiting only for the teacher to leave, and as soon as she leaves, no one can be seen in the class the next minute. Shivansh and Shweta are not in any hurry, but they get swept along with everyone else.

This has to be the first change in the past or rather the new life, he thinks. *The kid me didn't like Shweta but Shraddha. She was just a friend of mine. I can say that I admired her though, she was a model student, best in academics, such articulate speech with accurate pronunciation and bursting confidence and to top it all, firm grip over grammar, yet she had a kind and warm nature. She was not the best in sports though. I think everyone liked her. Maybe the admiration I had for her stopped me from liking Shweta romantically. Talking about liking, I am a 26-year-old dude in a 13-year-old body, does that make me a paedophile? Or age is just a number? No! I am only a 13-year-old boy, an early teen. I am normal, I am normal, or am I? Ugh!* He finally gives up after thinking for a while and thinks, *it is what it is... Though people in 2013 have to wait a couple of years to throw this word around on social media,* he grins.

Then he remembers Tushar, *that pipsqueak had a crush on Shweta, didn't he?* He can't remember the time, but he knows that they will become friends and at some point, further in the future he will talk about his feelings for Shweta to Shivansh. *But that's not a big deal,* he concludes. *For two big reasons, One, nothing happened, or should I say will happen between him and Shweta. And two, I can never forget even if I wanted to,* 'Back in the day I had this huge crush on you.' *Shweta said so herself to me even before we started dating.*

He is relieved and happy again after coming to such a happy conclusion. He then decides to act the way he did *back in the day* for the time being and goes to play basketball with his friends.

I think it would be best for me to behave the way I used to for the time being and let Shweta fall for me, he blushes. *I need to stop thinking about this while playing!* He screams in his head.

He starts to notice something the instant he starts focusing on the match. His body feels light and agile. The flexibility and reaction speed are way better than he is used to from his 26-year-old body, the only catch is that his reach is lesser, and he finds it hard to control this body of his, which he has long forgotten about. Obviously, this is all because he is now younger, which means better, better but shorter.

Slowly, he begins to take better control over his body as the game goes on. He regrets not playing regularly when he graduated from college and worked day and night at his new job, otherwise he could have had a far better body, he was just 26 after all. But everything is different now, he has this growing body and years of experience and skills in many games he has played. He knows tactics and strategies now unlike when he played purely on his instincts when he was younger. He realizes that his skills aren't as good as they were earlier but way better than an average 13-year-old.

Let's just win this one and think about the rest later, he thinks and begins to increase the pace of the game. As usual, his love for playing makes him forget everything else, and all he can think now is to score. He scores one basket after another, most of them are lay ups, some are two-pointers, and he is not even trying to throw a three-pointer as he has never been good with shooting anyway.

'You played great today! What did you have for breakfast?'

'Dude how did you manage that series of flukes?' someone laughs.

'Unbelievable man!'

Shivansh gets showered with a rain of comments, some genuine praises, and some only thinking about his extraordinary luck.

'I sure was lucky today,' says Shivansh trying to escape from the group and looking for the only one, Shweta. *What's she doing? Where is she? Did she see me play? If she did then I think I may have earned some points,* he laughs.

He tries to find her, he goes to the indoor games room then the volleyball court, back to the basketball court, and stairs around the court. He finally gives up on finding her and starts heading back to the classroom. He walks past the assembly ground and sees Shweta, surrounded by girls. They are bombarding her again with questions. Before she can answer one, someone throws another question at her so, she stays there awkwardly listening to everyone around her talk nonstop. *She was never into sports! I was so in-game that I forgot?* He thinks. *I just hope "that" happens soon.*

Eventually, something will happen somewhat related to school in which Shivansh and Shweta get to work together which means, spending some time together. Shivansh obviously has an idea about what's about to come.

I always asked her to send me her photos from childhood, I mean who wouldn't? Especially if one has such a cute girlfriend. She didn't send many but the ones she deemed worthy enough to send had me on cloud nine. A teacher for the next class enters and interrupts Shivansh's chain of thought. *Who could have imagined that I would get to see "kid" Shweta in front of me? But I guess I should focus on the lesson for now, I have some pride as a 26-year-old, soon to be 27 actually and I don't want to receive a nice crisp slap.* Shivansh tries his very best to avoid doing anything weird from this point on. Aside from some peeks at her, he manages to pass the class usually.

'Any plans for tomorrow?' asks Aakash.

'Nothing, till now. All students who live near the school have to come tomorrow for Independence Day, rest can sleep till whenever they want,' replies Shivansh.

'After that, idiot'

'Still same, nothing in mind right now. Any suggestions?'

'No…'

'All right! Let's just meet the day after tomorrow then,' says Shivansh thinking it will be easier for him to figure out what he needs to do further in the future if he has more time on his hands.

15th August 2013, cloudy weather. It can rain anytime. Everything is dimly lit with white light and looks beautiful. The gentle wind carries the scent of the newly bloomed flowers to everyone at the assembly ground. The flag hoists high, fluttering with the wind and releasing countless rose petals. The band starts to play, and everyone starts to sing the National Anthem in perfect sync at the top of their voices. "*Josh*" is high in these young students, even the loudest of thunder cannot break their rhythm. A box is handed to each student, and opening it reveals a *samosa,* a 200 ml *fruity,* a sweet, and some chips. *Memories…* Shivansh smiles feeling nostalgic. It takes a little more than two hours for the event to wrap up and everyone leaves for their homes. The school falls quiet.

Before I start planning, I think I should study first. That way I'll have fewer restrictions from mom and dad, as well as school. The amount of content that I have to learn is nothing in comparison to what I had to deal with in college. Let's just catch up with the syllabus till today and if I have enough time then I'll just cover more, Shivansh thinks.

The moment he is home, he goes straight to his study table and dives into his books. Focused.

'Shivansh, beta it's time for lunch', his mother calls him from the kitchen. He looks at the clock and finds that three hours have passed but he's happy with his progress. 'Yes maa, I'll be there in five…' his mother interrupts him, 'No five minutes! Come here right now, you eat so slow I don't want extra unwashed dishes in my sink.'

'*Hanji* I'll be there in a sec…' Shivansh doesn't wish to see his mother mad although he misses the way she used to scold him first and then console him saying that she doesn't like scolding him, but she loves him and does it only for his best interest, even though she's the one who suffers the most seeing him cry.

He goes into the kitchen, picks up a plate, and serves himself some *sabzi*. Now how can his mother not notice that her son who hates *sabzi* serving himself in the right amount for the first time?

'What has happened to you?' she asks.

Shivansh being completely oblivious has nothing to say. He looks at his mother suggesting that he has no idea what she's talking about.

'Nothing, go have your lunch,' she says.

Shivansh goes to sit in front of the television and takes a cross-legged position on the floor. His little brother is begging their father to watch anything but the news. He gives him a stare and Tarun stops speaking and gets back to the food with a glum face. Some people are arguing about who knows what on the television, basically it seems like a fish market. Pooja joins them and the whole family is now having lunch together. Shivansh missed this. One of the best things that is happening to him is the time he can spend with his family, getting to eat together, getting scolded, and fighting with his little brother over trivial stuff. Parents being parents noticed the changes Shivansh has shown all of a sudden but it's not like he is doing anything wrong, it's just that he is changed, slightly but changed. He is still the same Shivansh they know but more mature. They decide not to discuss this, *he must have realized his responsibilities as an elder brother and is trying his best to make us proud and set an example for Tarun,* they think. And decide not to poke him while he was trying so hard.

'How's everything at school? Are you prepared for your exams?' asks Pooja knowing what his answer would be, but it is hard not to ask anyway.

'Great Maa! I'm almost done with the syllabus and will start revision soon.'

'And how are you so quiet?' asks Vivek, who can't seem to hold it any longer.

'Well, you always say not to talk while eating…' says Shivansh not in a sarcastic way.

'Yeah… right. It's good that you finally get it. Tarun, you should learn from your brother!'

'Han Papa…' Shivansh sighs wondering how it always ends up like this.

Everyone picks up their plate and heads to the kitchen to keep them in the sink except the head of the family, Shivansh picks up his father's plate too. Pooja starts washing the dishes and

Shivansh stays there to talk to her for a while to keep her company.

'What will you do now? Have some rest, you can watch television or play on your computer for a while,' says Pooja after seeing him studying for hours.

'No, I'll finish the revision, and then can I go to play?'

'Fine, but don't get any kind of injury before your exams, okay?'

'Yeah, I'll be careful and there's time for exams.'

Shivansh gets back on his plan to conquer the syllabus and Tarun also has to study to stay safe from scolding, keeps staring at a book, waiting for an hour to finish so, he can ask to play some games. He does try to study for half of the time he keeps sitting. Right after exactly one hour he goes to Vivek and asks to play games on the computer, 'I promise I'll study before dinner too, please, please, please let me play some games.'

'Fine but only for half an hour, then you'll play outside,' even he can't resist the puppy eyes.

Another three hours and 53 minutes have passed, and Shivansh is done with all of the syllabus. Looks at the clock again to check if he can manage some time to play, the clock shows 05:30 pm, not too late to leave. He gets up takes a long breath and exhales, 'Maa, can I go now?' Pooja nods and he leaves without any delay.

'You are late!' says Anup, yes Anup not Anoop, that's how his name is spelled.

'Yeah, you know about the exams, right? It keeps harder and harder to ask to go outside. Had to study for hours then only I was allowed.'

'Yeah right, same story! Now join my team we are one player short.'

'I bet you guys are losing without me,' Shivansh chuckles.

'Hah, you wish! We are even at 18 to 18,' Anup smirks.

'The match just started; I am not that late then'

The match goes on. Shivansh keeps getting more and more familiar with his nimble body. As always Shivansh gets completely lost in the game and plays without holding back. After some solo plays and passes, he feels warmed up. The only handicap he has is his team, young students with almost no experience and tactics. The match ended with a one-sided victory, the score being 24 to 58 in favour of Shivansh's team. Some of the players in the losing team are pissed but can't say anything, it went fair and square. Winners or losers everyone invades Anup's house for water, adjacent to the basketball court. His mother serves them lemonade. Everyone leaves Anup at home and goes to the stairs. They want to talk for a while before they head home. The lights in the courts are switched on by a worker as it starts to get dark. Shivansh knows that he'll be in trouble if he doesn't leave soon.

'See you guys at school then…' he says as he gets up to leave.

Reaching home on time gets Shivansh some peace and no complaints from anyone. There's some time before dinner so he gets back to his desk. *Finally, some time to figure out what I have to do,* he thinks.

He makes up a list.

1. Some body weight training daily to gain some weight and strength. You skinny Shivansh! Change that!

2. Revision before exams, you don't want to score less and have a scolding over that.

3. Teach Tarun every once in a while, especially maths and science.

4. Keep track of the share market and cryptocurrency, why not earn some bucks while at it?

5. You are just a kid now! Who gets to live their childhood again? Have fun!

Some things are not on the list but are impossible not to remember. He knows now who his true friends are and what he did wrong in the past. He can now change everything. He can literally change his past. He wants to treat his mother the way she deserves and never make her sad, for anything. And lastly, the root of all the wickedness, to be with Shweta.

Shivansh knows that a growing body should have at least eight hours of sleep. He goes to bed early and lets Shweta roam freely in his head, he wants to keep thinking about her. Fatigue does catch up and makes his eyes harder to keep open, he goes to sleep with a smile.

CHAPTER 03: SNOW WHITE WITH HAZEL EYES

Buried under many layers of blanket, she wakes up on her mother's call. '*Bas* 5 minutes Mumma...' she asks in a sleepy voice while rubbing her puffed eyes. Still struggles to open her eyes as she pokes her face out and looks for her water bottle with one hand out of the blanket. She remains in bed for a couple of minutes. *Why is it so cold here all the time? Such a beautiful city ruined only by this weather;* she thinks. She was born and raised here and yet she is unable to cope with the cold. *Strange girl,* a common pronoun for her used by her friends.

Sadly, she needs to get up and go to school early in the morning and in such cold weather. Strengthening her nerves, she uncovers herself from the blankets, slowly, the way people test the water temperature with the tip of their toes before jumping in. It isn't even that cold at this time of the year but for her, it surely is. She rubs her arms with her hands to create a little bit of warmth. She wants to reach for the bus on time, and she hurries with everything but being clumsy she scuffles with countless hurdles.

Sitting on the bus that she nearly missed, she notices some noise but that doesn't bother her, what bothers her is that boy. The boy she saw in her new class on the first day. *Was he crying? I think he was looking at me. What could have made him cry anyway? Did something get into his eyes? I know what I saw; I wasn't daydreaming. He was crying, but why? And somehow, he looked happy, more than just happy, as if his dream had come true. What's with him weeping and smiling at the same time? He is the strange one!* She thinks.

Today is her second day at school and she can hear some students talking about him, the one that didn't seem normal.

'He is smart, isn't he,'

'He's good at sports too,'

'Did you see him play last time? He scored so many points,'

'He is nice, I talked to him once.' Listening to others talk about him right after she comes out of thinking about him makes her think about him more. *I guess everybody likes him,* she figures. All the gossip she hears about Shivansh starts to play in her head in a loop. She can tell that he is a good student, and performs well in academics and sports. Only making it harder for her to decode the look on his face when she entered the classroom for the first time.

The cold wind sluggishly leaks through the gaps in the windowpanes, the tyres make a creaky noise as the bus stops moving. She grabs the handle in front of her to avoid hitting her head in the next seat. She's at school.

'It'd be so nice if I had studied in this school from the start,' sighs Shweta as she steps down the bus, looking at the massive school building.

'Yeah, it must be awkward to change schools all of a sudden. It's hard making new friends, especially for you I think,' says Shraddha.

'Really, what makes you think that? You have known me only for one day,' says Shweta, shocked to see her accurate analysis.

'I can tell. Am I wrong?'

'No but still…'

'Yeah… let's just leave this. Tell me how come you change schools in the middle of the year?'

'It was my mum's idea; they made me join the school close to my home when I was little, but the catch is that it has only classes up to 10th standard. Sooner or later, I had to change schools…' interrupts Shraddha before she could complete.

'Lucky girl! You know what? Shivansh joined last year just like you.'

'Really? I had no idea,' Shweta asks in a louder tone than her usual in excitement.

'It looks like someone has a crush on someone,' teases Shraddha.

'It's nothing like that!' Shweta says with an unsteady voice, 'It's just that he seems… different, especially the way he acts. He is weird. You know when I entered the classroom yesterday, he was…' Shweta stops, *maybe telling her what I saw earlier isn't the best idea.* 'The point is I don't have a crush on him,'

'Yet…' says Shraddha again before she can complete.

'It's just that he is quite the character.' Says Shweta with her eyes wider.

'Okay, okay I get it. But will the other girls believe you?'

'Ms. Shraddha! You are not going to discuss this with others, am I clear?'

'Yeah, I'm just kidding don't get so serious early in the morning.' She replies.

'Talking about early mornings, God! Why do schools start so early? It's so hard to get up and come to school.'

They keep talking as they enter the gate. It is already time for assembly, and everyone is heading for the same. They go along with other girls, surprisingly enough, Shraddha doesn't mention Shivansh. Shweta exhales with relief. Soon, all the students and teachers gather in the hall and the prayer starts. Shweta looks for Shivansh, she tries her best not to be so obvious. Excluding Shweta and some other troublemakers, all the students have their eyes closed.

Some teachers are praying with their eyes closed including the principal, Mrs. Pushpa Sharma. She is not one of the best but the best principal the school has ever seen. She is admired by all the students and teachers. Her kindness has a unique charm, and she knows how to handle stress, by playing badminton with the students. She often manages some time to talk with students, she knows almost every student personally and remembers their names. She has such a positive energy surrounding her that can change the atmosphere of the room in an instant.

Some teachers are walking around, looking for those who are not praying properly.

'I can't hear you,'

'Keep your eyes closed,'

'You want to receive some kind of special treatment in front of everyone?' they often used to tell to keep students in check. They also keep a sharp eye for latecomers so, no one can come late and join the assembly unnoticed and unpunished. Students hate these teachers.

After prayer, everyone pays attention to the rest of the assembly. Shweta still cannot find him. Another half an hour passes, and everyone heads to the classes. *So, what if he didn't come?*

I don't even know him, and it's been only two days since I started coming to this school. Then why am I getting annoyed just because he didn't care enough to come to school? It must be something else. Maybe I'm not feeling well today, maybe I just miss my old school. Something in her keeps telling her that he is the reason for all her anxiousness and frustration, but she doesn't want to admit it. How can she? It is all so random for her.

'Hey,' she gets summoned back from her realm of thoughts.

'Hey Shweta, you are feeling all right?'

'Yes, I'm fine. What do you want?' she snaps but then realizes the one in front of her is Shivansh himself. *God! Where were you?*

'I'm sorry, I was just thinking about… something.' She is mad at herself for behaving this way.

'Yeah, it's all right,' Shivansh is just happy to make an excuse to talk to her.

'You are not sick, are you?' he asks with genuine concern. This suddenly makes Shweta feel better, though she doesn't know why.

'No, I am fine really'

'Okay, must be lost in thoughts...Anyway Shweta, just to inform you, your roll number is 36. And the first period is free today. So, if you *really* are fine then I can show you the school if you want...'

'Why are you telling me this and offering me a tour? Are you the class monitor?' she says sarcastically but soon realizes that it can be true. She does want to go with him, but she doesn't want to make it too easy for him to talk to her or have a walk with her, this early.

'Yes'

'What?'

'Yes, I am the class monitor and I don't have anything to do so, I thought I could help you out. Shraddha is doing some homework she was supposed to do yesterday. I can ask her or someone else to show you around if you want.'

'Okay, sorry I didn't know and thank you for offering help. Can you show me around?' she asks politely to hint that she is fine with him walking around the school. The one thing she doesn't want to happen is her cheeks getting red. *Oh my god! Not Now!*

They head out.

'You already know the one thing you must know, right?'

'Girl's washroom? Yes, I know.'

'Good, now I don't have to…'

They both laugh softly; they can sense that they can talk easily without any awkwardness despite how she reacted earlier. She keeps walking beside him as he keeps telling her about the school. She's amazed that he's not only talking about where's what but also drags her into every room to introduce her to the teachers. *Thank God it's such a small school!*

'This is our library, and he is our head librarian and he's also the advisor of Reader's Club, Mr Manoj,' he tells her as they approach Mr Manoj and then turns to him and introduces Shweta, 'Sir, this is Shweta, a new student.'

'This is our computer lab, and he is Mr. Krishna. Sir, this is Shweta, a new student.'

'This is our Music room, and he is Mr. Pradeep. Sir, this is Shweta, a new student'

'Hello Shweta, welcome to our school.'

'Thank you, sir.' She feels a little weird about the way he is handling the school tour, but she also feels nice, somehow. After such a long tour to personally meet and greet every teacher at school, she feels her throat getting dry and her legs want to walk no more.

Shivansh knows her ability to handle something physical. He is even amazed to see her walk around so much and climb up and down the stairs with him. He asks her to take a small break.

'Let me show you our cafeteria,' She follows him and rests on a chair hoping for something to drink.

Shivansh gets her a glass of water. Seeing her gulping so fast, he asks if she wants to drink more but she nods her head with some water still in her mouth. He goes back and drinks a glass himself and puts the paper glass in the bin. He orders two cheap coffees and two cheaper burgers and brings everything to the table. He really wants to see her eat a burger. He just loves how she eats; he can recall a short video of her eating something from back in those adult days.

'So, how was the tour?

'It was nice, sort of… You said you'd show me around but didn't tell me that you would introduce me to every teacher in the school. Like

OH MY GOD! What even was that!' they laughed. 'I know it's a small school and there are only about 30 teachers here but still…'

'So, you are saying that you didn't like it?'

'I didn't say *that*… but it was weird.'

'Weird?'

'Different, I mean.'

'And you don't like different?'

'C'mon stop this!' says Shweta laughing.

'Yeah, I am just messing with you. Well, this is me…'

She cannot make herself come and say it in his face but she liked their weird/different little tour. She liked getting introduced to teachers. She loved getting introduced to those little kids calling her, "Didi, Didi." She felt somewhat sorry for them that they had to come to school at such a young age but they were so cute, she loved meeting them.

Cute, he is cute, she thinks. She cannot decide if it is him or the kids that are cuter.

'You are good with kids,' she finally managed to find something to speak.

'Not just with kids. You'll see.'

'Okay, I shall then,' she smiles.

Then he takes her to the terrace close to the cafeteria. The wind takes the fragrance of the lake and hits them unprepared. Her hair starts to move in a hypnotic way that takes his breath away. He cannot move further like he is being strangled by some spell. He wants to touch her hair but cannot lift his hand. She starts to grab her hair, which stops the spell cast on Shivansh. He can breathe now. They both then witnessed the view now that the sudden wind gets gentler. The view is phenomenal here, like always. They can see the Nainital Lake; no one is boating at this time of the day. Only to be touched by the wind, which makes small ripples in it. Two hills behind the lake meet at the bottom, and another hill larger than the two stands behind their junction. Some clouds are floating only to make everything look prettier as if someone has intentionally made them stick there to portray the beauty of calmness.

'Isn't it nice here?'

'Yeah...' she says with some hint of not being flabbergasted.

Shivansh could easily tell that her words didn't deliver what she thought, 'You don't find this beautiful?'

'I do, it's not like I don't like this, but the thing is I have lived here my whole life, and scenes like this are all I see almost every day. It is pretty but quite boring for me...'

'Okay, I didn't know if anyone can get bored of mountains and hills and views like this.'

He doesn't say anything after that, neither does she reply to him. Shweta looks out aimlessly and Shivansh looks at the mountains far away and steals every third second to look at her. She goes to a nearby bench and sits. He just looks at her move and takes a seat, waits for a couple of seconds, and sits closer to her, wondering what's going through her mind. He is still not sure what to say to her but they both find the silence soothing so, they keep sitting in silence. Shivansh has stopped looking at the mountains, all his eyes see is Shweta. Shweta breaks the sweet silence.

'Why are you looking at me like that?'

'Because you are beautiful. I enjoy looking at beautiful people,' Shivansh couldn't resist.

'What?' She is shocked and turns red, completely red.

'Wait, wait, wait. You have read *The Fault in Our Stars*, haven't you?' he asks.

'No, why?'

Of course, she hasn't! You idiot! She will read that book later in her life. Don't forget stuff like this! He thinks. 'So, what I just said is from a novel, *The Fault in Our Stars*. It's a must-read and I'm sure you'll love it.'

'How'd you know?' she tries to raise one eyebrow to make an interrogative face. She fails, fails hard. All Shivansh can see is her struggling and making cute expressions.

'I just know…' he says trying to suppress his laughter.

Bell rings, not with the slow timed hits to intimate the beginning of the next period but with nonstop fast-paced hitting to indicate it's time for a lunch break.

'This was the first time I ever bunked,' says Shweta.

'Same. And three periods straight! Too much even for veterans.'

'Really? I don't think so.'

'Not kidding. With you, time just flew by.'

'Not bad, not bad. Now you'll tell me that this is your first time hitting on a girl too.'

'I'm, I'm not hitting on you, I just stated that while I was with you...' he pauses, 'Okay, it does sound like I *am*,' he says, scratching the back of his head and giving off a smile of slight shyness.

'It's fine,' she assures, 'I had fun.'

'What's fine? Like you were just messing with me "fine", or I can hit on you "fine"?' he chuckles, trying to give her a counter.

'Shivansh!' she squints her eyes.

'But what you just said. That does make you sound like you are hitting on me.'

'Whatever,' she rolls her eyes at Shivansh, amazed by his audacity.

'So, what do you have for lunch? I am starving, let's head back.'

'I don't know, will see.'

'You'll most probably eat with your friends and won't be bunking the rest of the periods, right?'

'Obviously!' They laugh as they leave the bench and head back to their classroom.

'So, Shweta, how was your first day?'

'Nice, I made some new friends, liked the school...' she takes a short pause, 'and everything else,' says softly.

They share a friendly smile as they go their separate ways.

Shivansh jumps in delight to see *Aloo ke Parathe* in his lunch box. He selfishly shares the smallest bites with his friends and begins to enjoy his meal all by himself. His eyes again look for Shweta, she is also eating with her friends. She looks cute, like a squirrel, the way she looked while they were eating the burgers. Nevertheless, she is eating in a calm and composed manner, her dining etiquette makes her look even cuter. While Shivansh is eating and talking and laughing. He chews his food slowly and with his lips sealed, barely qualifying as etiquette.

She likes it, every time Shivansh looks at her. Even she tries to steal a glance at him, every once in a while, when no one is looking at her. Shivansh finishes his lunch but is still talking, which Shweta notices.

Is he not going to wash his hands? Thinks Shweta, is always concerned with hygiene. Another minute or two pass and she leaves after completing her lunch. Her friends are still busy talking but she cannot waste another second to wash her hands. On the way she hears Shivansh's voice, 'I'll be back in five, gotta wash my hands.' She turns back to check if he's coming and continues to walk. Shivansh walks faster to catch up to her and walk side by side. They start washing their hands. *Her hands, can they be any cuter?* He asks himself. *They are so small! Just a 4-year-old, and so white, I can even trace arteries in her hands.* He cannot forget how it felt to hold them. He even remembers the first time they held hands and when he was playing with her hands while she was on a phone call. He remembers feeling her pulse rising so high that he could literally feel it. It was faint but he could hear her heart pounding intensely on his touch. The moment he told her about it, she swiftly pulled her hand back in embarrassment.

'Your hands, they are so freakishly small,' he says after he forces himself to come back to the present with superhuman effort.

'Yeah, aren't they cute? I love my hands.' *God! Did he just mention my hands? Does he like them? Or does he find them funny-looking? Shivansh, why are you taking so long to reply? Say something! Fast! Now!*

'Yes, they are, unlike mine.' *She really is the Shweta I know, she said the same thing she used to say back then, all the time. How is this girl so obsessed with her hands so much? I thought I was the weird one to find her hands so attractive.* He raises his hands to let Shweta have a better look. 'They are already this big and I know they'll get even bigger.' They share a quick laugh.

'I guess the lunchtime is about over.'

'Yeah, anytime now.'

They start to walk back. 'Okay then, until next time.' He says as they enter the class once again.

They didn't know that that was the last time they'd get to talk that day. The teachers kept coming at the right time in each period, not giving any time to talk leisurely. The last period is over, and everyone is rushing to get home or their favourite seat on the bus. Shweta feels a little unsettled and frustrated, *the worst part is that I know exactly why I feel like this. It's because of him!* She shakes her head and starts moving to get the bus before it leaves.

He didn't say anything after that. Anything. She keeps thinking. *Why do I feel like this? Ugh! I get that he is nice to me, maybe he's like that with everyone else too. Maybe it's just me who's thinking like that. Maybe it just happened in a way that we got to talk so much in the morning and in the same way it just happened that we didn't get to talk after that. Maybe he does want to talk to me or maybe he doesn't. Ugh! This is so confusing! Let's try one thing, I am not gonna think about this, about him, for now, and wait to see what happens tomorrow.* She tries to leave all her tension and confusion to the next day and takes a seat, not the one she wanted. She cannot be any more impatient to get home and just throw herself on her bed, but the bus is still not full, which means she has to wait longer.

She hates it. *What's with today? It started so great like I was flying, and we lost track of time. We were having so much fun and look at it now, could it be any worse? First, we didn't even get to talk after lunch and now waiting for this stupid bus to start moving.* After one of the lengthiest eight minutes, the bus slowly starts moving to get out of the parking. The bus turns right, she is sitting on the left window seat. There he is, sitting on a bench, with his friends. Their eyes meet, and he raises his hand waves at her and whispers "bye" without making a sound. She "hears" him and waves back at him, trying to be as obscure as possible. He can see the prettiest smile on her face and wonders what made her so happy, little does he know that he is the one who just flipped her mood.

On the way back, she jumps up and down but only in her head, she maintains a controlled smile on her face, trying not to look too cheerful to make others ask what's the reason. Her head is completely filled with Shivansh, she knows this but she doesn't want to stop thinking about him. It's been just a day but somehow, he made her feel like he had known her for a very long time. He didn't do anything obvious, but she could feel he cared for her.

The bus stops for the third time, it's time for Shweta to leave the bus and take a short walk to her house. But she cannot stop thinking even though there's so little to think about. She goes to her room and covers herself with blankets, *God! I was just waiting for this the whole day.* She cannot sleep though. She is tired from roaming across the school the whole day and has so much to think about, but she just cannot sleep yet.

She tries turning sideways and burying her face in the pillow, but nothing seems to work. After struggling for quite some time, exhaustion catches up and the thoughts about Shivansh begin to grow quieter, she begins to fall slowly into sleep, under the warmth of many blankets. The last thought that came to her mind was, *how am I supposed to talk to him tomorrow? How am I supposed to behave, to say?*

On the other edge of the city, there is someone else having trouble sleeping, that boy is Shivansh. Countless thoughts keep running wild through his mind, thoughts about someone special, he is not the same boy who travelled back in time. He is a teen now, a teen in love. This girl has his heart and mind. Again. *Did she enjoy or get bored of me? I know I went a little over the top with the school intro, but it was fun. I think. Did she think I was weird? How will she talk to me tomorrow? Will she talk to me at all? Is she even thinking about me, even a fraction of how much I am thinking about her? STOP! Shivansh, you need to stop now. It's getting a little too much, but it was never less than a little too much, to begin with. Damn! I'm in love with her again.* He slaps his forehead and smiles. *No matter how many lives I get to see her again, I'll fall for her every single time. I don't know how big of an idiot I was back when I didn't see her the way I do now, I was just next to her, I mean Shraddha is a nice girl to date but can any girl in the world come close to my Shweta? No, I know that. At least for me. Okay, you seriously need to stop now and sleep.* He shuts his eyes and stops moving.

He tries his best to keep his mind sane and his heart less loud. Futile. He keeps changing sides, his eyes just refuse to stay shut.

He tries to bore himself to sleep by studying but that doesn't work either. He tries to count but he has reached somewhere around 2,453 and still can't see a hope to get some sleep. The last time he checked the time, it was 2 o'clock! But silently the sleep creeps on him and he closes his eyes with a smile.

How am I supposed to talk to her tomorrow? How am I supposed to behave, to say?

CHAPTER 04:
A DATE, SORT OF

Unlike his usual morning routine, this is the second time in recent days that Shivansh cannot get up. He kept turning left and right thinking about her till he finally lost all his energy and slept, he could see why he was so out of energy and in no mood to get up.

'Bittu,' Pooja calls him in the sweetest voice in the world.

'Get up now, couldn't sleep last night? I saw when you turned on the lights in the middle of the night.'

'Good morning, Maa,' Shivansh yawns while covering his mouth with one hand and stretching out the other upward.

'I couldn't sleep so, I tried to study for a while. Did I wake you up? I'm Sorry maa I didn't want to.'

'Don't worry beta, tell me if you are not feeling well. Want to go to school today?'

'Yes, I can go to school.' Shivansh jumps out of bed and gulps down the whole glass of water his mother is holding for him. It is easier for him to open his eyes now, and he slowly walks towards the bathroom.

It took him 45 minutes instead of 30 to get ready for school. He is doing everything at a slower pace, including breakfast. One thing he is not aware of has come to Pooja's notice. He is unusually happy today, a smile is stuck on his face, making his cheek slightly pink. Nevertheless, Pooja decides not to ask him anything. She is just happy to see his son happy. What Shivansh is aware of is the noise his heart is making, just thinking about her makes his heart go crazy. How can he not worry about his mother hearing his heart racing if she just gets close enough?

Lack of sleep causes Shivansh to do everything slower including arriving late at school. He successfully manages to sneak past the radar of teachers finding the students not doing the prayer in an ideal way. He hides his bag behind a pillar and inconspicuously joins his class's queue, joins his hands with his eyes closed begins to sing the prayer with the others. Once he has confirmed that he is safe now, he opens one eye and looks for Shweta, it isn't easy to get a clear sight of a girl who's standing in fourth place from the front in the girls' queue. He is back in the second last place in the boys' queue, he cannot look at her face without moving, at least not while praying.

Little does he know what goes in her mind, *where is he? Why is he late again? Is he even coming today? Is he all right? He is not sick, is he? Ugh! Where is he?* She is again wearing braids today. *I liked the loose hair from yesterday, the way they danced in the wind, just makes you go numb,* he thinks. *But she does look cute wearing the champu braids style,* he smiles.

Both are not wholly present where they are supposed to be. After the assembly, they start to get flown with the rest of the students, to their classroom. She reaches before Shivansh does and takes her seat. Being the bookworm she is, she takes a book out of her bag without even noticing what she is doing. Her head is somewhere else yet, a book lies on her desk open. *Did he really not come today? What is wrong with him? I couldn't sleep last night; it took so much of my willpower to get out of bed to come to school. If it wasn't for him, I wouldn't have come. Stupid!* He walks in. Out of all the eyes, he finds her eyes in an instant. She feels her eyes getting drawn to her left, towards the door, only to find him stupidly looking at her. Her mind tells her to stop doing the same but she cannot help but look back at him, in his eyes. He notices some restlessness in her eyes, how can he possibly know that she couldn't sleep last night, just like him? The moment is not bound to be ruined by time or sound but by Shraddha. She taps Shivansh's shoulder gently to bring him back to the class and says, 'Don't get so lovey-dovey first thing in the morning Shivansh.'

'What?' says Shivansh, not knowing how to respond to something like that.

'I said, "Don't get so lovey-dovey first thing in the morning Shivansh."'

'I heard that. I asked what do you mean by that?'

'Oh so, you don't know what I am talking about. Okay, I'll tell Shweta you don't like her at all.'

Shivansh decides not to open his mouth, anything could backfire in front of her. He is still figuring out a way to deal with her when she leans slightly towards him and whispers, 'Don't worry your secret's safe with me but if you two keep acting so stupidly then I don't think the secret will remain a secret for long.' Shivansh just nods and goes to his seat. *I should have just told her that I saw a monkey through the window or something. But not saying something is better than saying something stupid.*

The 40-minute class felt like an eternity in hell, some of it was because of lack of sleep and most of it was to see her from afar and not being able to go to her, talk to her, and just be next to her. The next teacher arrives early, even before the previous one could leave, not allowing Shivansh to talk to Shweta. Mrs Rekha leaves and Mr Chanchal starts his class without wasting a single second. Shivansh realizes that the more he wants to talk to her the harder it becomes.

With each passing minute, thinking nothing but about her, Shivansh feels ravished to hear the unpleasant sound of the bell for lunch. *Finally! Who's gonna stop me now?* His own friends stop him. Not caring worth a dime what is going on in Shivansh's head, they drag him out to play basketball with the little time they are left with after having lunch. He can't even make any excuse, he always used to play in the lunchtime with nothing else to do. He can't dig his own grave by telling everyone that all he wants to do with his time is to just talk to her. *I guess I can tell Aakash. If I tell anyone else, then they won't let me live in peace and they'd tell the girls too. I don't think Shweta can handle that. Ugh! If I could then I would shout in front of the world that I love her, and that the universe gave me another chance to prove my love and be with her. Focus on the present now, Shivansh! Think about what you can do now.*

Like a guest, she remains silent with her friends throughout the break. With no plausible reason, he can't make his way out of the basketball match. His mind is somewhere else, he keeps making stupid mistakes while playing. He can't help but see himself losing the game. He doesn't even want to play; he just wants to get back to Shweta.

Coming back to his class after losing the match does feel bad. *Couldn't talk to her and now losing a match. Why can't I just get a little time to just have a chat with her?* He goes to his seat and sits with his head lowered in anger. He is aimlessly looking at the ground and his left elbow carries the weight of his head. Shweta sees him and can feel how frustrated he is right now. She gives Shraddha a "look". Shraddha takes the mission with high spirits and says, 'Let's head outside for a while, the break will be over soon. Shweta, are you coming or are you still not feeling good?'

'I guess I'll just stay here,' says Shweta, trying to hide her smile.

She waits for others to leave; the moment they leave the door she gets up and goes to Shivansh. Takes the seat in front of him facing him but he's still unaware of her presence next to him.

'What happened Shivansh?' she asks with genuine care for him.

Shivansh is awe-struck by the soothing voice he hears; he cannot believe Shweta has come to him. He slowly turns his face up to get a look at her face, trying to hide his joy, he cannot let her know how happy he is now just to see her, and he has forgotten why he was so frustrated in the first place. His eyes fall on her glittering lips that can radiate happiness in his heart with just a smile at him. As he gazes higher and higher, he can see her naturally blushing cheeks, a small nose, and eyes that are smiling but with a hint of worry for Shivansh. She is right next to him, holding the backrest of the bench and resting her chin on her hand.

Say something, Shivansh! A voice screamed in his head. *What am I supposed to say? I heard her but what did she ask me? I have no idea. Can't believe how cute she is. She is right in front of me. Why did she come here? Is she asking something about the last class? I hope not. Damn! I can keep looking at her eyes forever. Think Shivansh think! Why did she come here? Wait can't I just ask her? Yes, I can do that. Let's just ask her and see how it goes.*

'Sorry, what did you say? I was thinking about something...'

'Mr Shivansh, I just asked you about what happened to you. Where's your smile? But I think I was worried for nothing. Look at you now. I think you are just hiding it.'

Did she just come here to cheer me up? Did she notice my bad mood? It feels so good if someone cares enough to come and ask about what had happened, just because they can tell that my mood is not the best. Of course, I forgot what I was sad about! I mean look at you, coming here, just for me. What more do I need to be happy? All I wanted was to talk to you, from the start. Now I can finally see you up close.

'Some stuff happened but I am good now. In fact, I'm great,' he says with an eye-to-eye smile.

'Now tell me what really happened?' she squints her eyes.

'I'm telling Shweta, nothing happened, I had trouble sleeping last night then I got late to school, and then lost the match just now.'

'You too? Even I couldn't sleep last night.'

'Why? What happened?' he asks with worrying eyes.

'Nothing…' she can't bring herself to tell him that he's behind everything weird happening to her these days, he kept running through her mind and keeping her on her toes.

'There's always a *something* behind every nothing.' He chuckles.

'Shut up, stupid!' She says to hide her embarrassment.

'Okay so, I am stupid now, but even someone stupid can tell that you just dodging the question.'

'So? I won't tell if I don't want to.'

'Okay, okay, madam! You don't have to. Happy?'

'By the way, why didn't *you* sleep?' she smirks.

'If I tell you then will you tell me too?'

'No.'

'That's convenient!'

They both laugh. They talk a little more and then she returns to her seat, Shivansh watches her as she gets up from the seat next to him, takes some steps, turns back, and raises her hand only up to her waist level to wave at him. She walks back clumsily and hits her toe with the bench next to her. Shraddha could not hold her friends out any longer and if they saw her talking to Shivansh like that, they would jump to all kinds of conclusions and handling them is a little too much for her.

Unlike the whole day, luck takes their side for once and the girls return right after Shweta takes her seat. Shraddha did her job splendidly. She looks at Shivansh, he is smiling. She then looks at Shweta, only to find her smiling with a little blush. *Mission accomplished;* she thinks.

She goes to Shivansh and asks, 'You were not so cheerful when we left but now look at you, what happened?'

Shivansh becomes bashful, he averts his eyes and says, 'Nothing.'

'Don't worry, like I told you, your little secret is still a secret.'

'Thanks, Shraddha, and thanks for what you just did.'

'It's called investing,' she chuckles.

'Sure, anything, anytime, you just have to ask.'

Next teacher rushes in and Shraddha goes back to her seat. She sits next to Shweta; she whispers something to her and then they both look at Shivansh. Shivansh looks back at them, Shraddha laughs, and Shweta turns as red as a cherry. He tries hard to guess what Shraddha must have said to make Shweta blush so hard, but he is happy even not knowing about it, he knows it must be something about him and her.

The rest of the day goes as swiftly as anyone can imagine but for Shivansh, everything is moving in slow motion. He is busy gazing at Shweta evading the sharp eyes of every teacher.

Shweta is trying her best to steal a few looks at him and then instantly gets back to the blackboard not giving him enough time to lock their eyes. This little game of theirs' goes on till it's about time for everyone to go home but for some reason, Shivansh is no longer looking at her.

All of a sudden, he becomes a nerd and starts to take notes. He is completely focused on what he is writing, he hasn't looked up since the moment he started writing, neither at the board nor at her. He continues to write even after the bell has rung. Puts a full stop at the end and looks up to find the class almost empty.

His eyes again meet hers as she passes by the door to leave the classroom. He quickly throws everything in his bag, grabs his bag in one hand and the notebook in another, and gets up. *No, no, keep writing. Why are you getting up?* Thinks Shweta and leaves before he can.

He starts running towards the bus stand where Shweta is supposed to come to get the bus home. On the way, he rips the page he was writing on for the last 10 minutes and puts the notebook back in his bag. He folds the page in half and waits for her to arrive. Shweta comes with her friends at a regular pace, looking where

Shivansh must have run to every few seconds. Her eyes widen as she catches Shivansh waiting for her there, but she cannot go and talk to him, all her friends are right by her side. Shivansh hopes that she gets her usual window seat and to his delight she does. He moves closer to her slowly, slowly enough not to get noticed by anyone else, and passes the page to her. She takes her hand out of the window and tries to stealthily grab the page, being the clumsy girl, she is. Nevertheless, she successfully takes the note without anyone else noticing.

She looks back, at Shivansh, as the bus takes her away from him. By the time the bus has moved so far ahead that she can no longer see him, she looks at the page she grabbed without even thinking.

Hey Shweta, you know who wrote this, don't you? So, the thing is I have a match this Sunday at the cricket ground in the city and I think you live close by. The match starts at 10 and I think it'll be over by 1. And then I was hoping you could help me get some stationary in the market...

> Actually, it's just an excuse. You know how hard it is to talk in school. It was so sweet of you to come and ask me how I was doing, was I really that obvious?
>
> Please come if it's all right with you. I'll just hope that you come but you don't have to, only if you feel like so. I know you can't tell me if you will come or not, don't worry I'll just wait for a while and if you don't show up then I will leave.

The first thought that comes to her mind is, *he took that long to write just this? Stupid.* She smiles.

She's happy, everyone on the bus is happy. After all, it's Saturday, no school tomorrow but something else makes her slightly happier than the rest. It means she can sleep however long she wants. She isn't much into sports, but the many other kids will be playing small one-day tournaments that will be managed by the kids themselves. Kids from all the nearby schools would come and make the weekend worthwhile.

Shivansh has no means of knowing how Shweta spends her Sundays, he can only hope for her to come. He decides that he will wait for her after the match and if she cannot come then he will not have any other option than leaving. Snapping back to reality he finds himself staring at his door, rings the bell, and says, 'Maa it's me.'

As usual, he goes out to play with his friends in the evening. He returns on time, just before it gets dark. He is exhausted today, lack of sleep from last night began to show its effect on his face. His head is still filled with thoughts, thoughts of her. *Will she come? I don't even have a clue what she used to do in her free time. Maybe she reads, maybe she watches some movies or something else, but I do believe she does not go out to play. How long will she stay, if she does come? Am I even going to say something to her? I hope I don't sit silently in front of her. You can do this Shivansh. You nailed it last time, right? Why are you even thinking about this? You have already decided what you are going to do. So, stop overthinking about this! She is not going to come anyway, is she? Shivansh, stop!*

It's 9 o'clock in the morning. A tiny beam of sunlight sneaks past a hole in the curtain and makes Shivansh cover his face. He has slept well, he feels refreshed and looks up at the clock and finds that he is going to be late for his match.

'Maa, why didn't you wake me up?'

'It's Sunday beta, and I was about to. Breakfast's ready. Hurry up and get ready. You have a match, don't you? You know I won't let you leave with an empty stomach.'

'You should have said so sooner.' He jumps off the bed and starts rushing with everything just to make it in time. *I don't know if she is coming, I don't want to be late for the match. I can't afford two losses in a row.*

He reaches the ground 25 minutes late. All he could think about was her on his way. He enters the gate and starts walking towards his friends. Suddenly, the way the brightest star overwhelms everything else on a moonless night, he cannot help but notice her sitting on a bench. He feels limitless happiness coursing through his entire body. He doesn't even know how to express what he is feeling, he is completely awe-struck. *She's always like this. I don't know how she manages to do something so sweet at the most unbelievable times. How can I not fall for her?*

This is just the second time; I would fall for her even if I were to come back a thousand times.

His friends' stares at him from the benches drag him back to reality. He tries his best to not look in her direction and goes to his team. The match was supposed to start at 10 so, everyone should have arrived at least an hour earlier. Luckily, they won the toss, and the captain chose to bat first. This means that even if he had arrived on time all he'd be doing is to sit on the bench and wait for his turn to bat.

He tells them how he could not get up on time and arrived late. Since the match has already started, no one is interested in giving him a cold shoulder. Now he can focus on the match. He starts to observe the nuances of the conShraddhaon of the ground and the opponent's behaviour to deduct a possible strategy that they might have picked. If he can accurately predict their moves, then it'd be easy to counter them and steal a victory.

Aakash jolts Shivansh to bring his attention back to the match again. Shivansh cannot believe he let his thoughts wander away from the present. *She came here even before the match started; I clearly remember telling her that the match would start at 10.* This small gesture means a lot to him. It forced him to relive the moment that had changed his life before he came back in time.

About a month had passed since they started dating each other. It was just another regular day, and they were talking over a phone call, after a while the conversation moved in a way that they started discussing about confession of love in movies and web series. From there they started discussing who would say the three magical words first.

'Is that even a question? It doesn't matter who says *it* first, right?' said Shivansh.

'All I know is that I am not going to be the one who says *it* first,' replies Shweta.

'Sure?'

'Absolutely! Don't even have a hint of doubt over this.'

'Okay let's see and even if you don't say it first, I just hope that when and if I say *it* first you won't be saying things like "What took you so long? You made me wait for such a long time"'

'In your dreams,' Shivansh can imagine her smirking.

After that, they never really talked about it again but the event that changed the course of Shivansh's life came about three months later, sooner than he could have ever imagined. He couldn't forget the day even if he wanted to, it was the 27th of November. It certainly wasn't the nicest day for Shweta, everything that came around her kept getting worse and kept irritating her. First, she couldn't sleep well, then she got up late and missed her bus to college, walked nearly three kilometres and so on and the day had just started. She told him everything. Shivansh wants to do something for her, something that can lift her mood, but he has no time. It was time to leave for college.

He quickly rendered a simple video with a few nice words and a background song and sent it to her. When he looked at the clock, he found out that he was getting late. So, before she could respond to the video, he left his room with a text saying, I hope that this makes your day just a little better.

He kept checking his phone again and again when he reached the college, but she still hadn't looked at the video, she didn't even come online. To top it off, while listening to her and making up the video he forgot to charge his phone, so his phone died, at the worst possible time. He couldn't get more frustrated but there was nothing he could do. *I'll reach home and plug in my phone and let's just hope that her mood gets a little better. Maybe she might have already seen it and sent me something like "Thank you, it made me feel much better."* That day, time seemed to move slower than a snail for Shivansh and college was much more boring than it usually was. By the time he reached home, it was already 8 o'clock, and the anticipation of Shweta's reply had long gone. He threw his bag in the corner and dived into his bed, plugged in his phone, and turned it on. Little did he know, she didn't send just a little "thanks", but he was blown away when he saw the numerous notifications popping up on his phone just from her. He quickly opened the messaging app and saw her texts.

---

video1.mp4

I hope that this makes your day just a little better…

> Shivansh yaar 😊 ♥♥ 💕
>
> YOU make me happy 💕 💕
>
> Just a second back my day
>
> was so shitty… but then this 💕 💕 💕
>
> And yeah
>
> Do you love me?
>
> Whatever you may think
>
> But
>
> I
>
> LOVE
>
> YOUUU
>
> !!!
>
> Been thinking about this for a while… but me being me, how could I, right? Then I thought this was the best opportunity
>
> Now that I have said this, I need at least 15 minutes to come out of the shock that this daring feat I did.

And just like that day, Shweta has again made an unexpected yet sweet gesture today. She is completely unaware that she has won him all over again.

He begins to see Aakash shouting at him, asking him to take the bat and to bat, one wicket is already down. The match is not going in their favour as much as they hoped. Opponents are far more experienced and familiar with the ground. Since they live nearby, they play on this ground daily while Shivansh and his friends come to this side of the city only on weekends.

One thing he could bet on was the stamina and tenacity of his team so, he came up with a strategy to stretch the match as much as they could. He goes to the other batsman and tells him to stay on the wicket as long as he can. He thinks that the longer they stick to the pitch, by any means possible, the more the opponents will grow restless. At the same time, the sun will continue to drain their energy as it rises with time. He is in a great dilemma; he just wants to get out and go to Shweta, but he can't just lose a match, especially in front of her. What option does he have except to win the match against any odds? He tries with a superhuman effort to concentrate on the bowler and not Shweta.

Shivansh takes the stance and is ready to face his first ball in the match, the bowler talks to his captain about something, and Shivansh, unable to hold his urge, looks at Shweta. She is looking at him, only him and only he can decipher the way Shweta cheers for him in her way, without showing any kind of gesture or saying anything. *I can see what you are doing there,* he thinks and locks his eyes back on the bowler who is ready to throw the ball.

The team managed to keep three wickets safe till the end of the innings and set a score of 178. Shivansh remains not out with 61 runs; his experience paid off in this match. The score isn't superb but also isn't too easy to beat, they have a chance to win. Aakash and others tease him the moment he takes a seat.

He can see that his strategy has worked out so far. It's now their turn to bowl, the opponent has a decent target of 179 in 20 overs. Shivansh sends most of the fielders near the boundary, he intends to let them have some extra singles and doubles and minimize the boundaries. This will continue to drain their already depleted stamina, and some forced attempts for boundaries may even result in some bonus catches.

It is now 1: 40 pm. 35 runs in 7 balls. The match, at this point, is in complete favour of Shivansh's team. They try to score sixes at every next ball, another two wickets down and they lose by 23 runs.

By 2:20 pm everyone leaves the ground except Shivansh and Shweta.

'You, Mr Shivansh, are very late!' says Shweta as Shivansh goes to sit next to her.

'Sorry,' replies Shivansh in a dry voice, still breathing slightly heavily. 'But I had to do this, to win this match you know. I think we got lucky, I thought we'd lose so I just tried my best to avoid a crushing defeat but look at my team! They played great, didn't they?'

'"I thought we'd lose," says who just won by more than 20 runs, not out at that,' she says trying to mimic Shivansh and handing him the water bottle from her bag. He laughs so hard; it is his first time seeing her or anyone mimicking him. Shweta looks like the cutest being on earth while acting.

'So, what do we do now? And why did you come so early? I told you the match would end around one. You came even before the match started and I remember telling you that it'd start at 10, if you had to see the match then you could've come around 10…'

'Well, I had nothing to do anyway. You decide where to go, don't you have some things to buy?'

'Then let's go to the stationary shop first and I have to buy some veggies too. Do you have something to buy too?'

'Yes, only a few things and even those are non-essentials.'

'All right let's get going then,' gives her bottle back, half empty.

'We can wait for a while if you are tired.'

'Not that I'm tired or anything but we can sit here for a while. Nobody's here, the weather is nice, and the ground, see the way the grass is moving with the wind.'

'Sure, Mr *I'm not tired.*' she does it again, and they both laugh.

10 minutes have passed, and they both are silent. Shweta has been looking at the grass dancing the way Shivansh told her, and Shivansh has been looking at her. He was right when he said that the weather was nice. The clouds have

come. The wind moves the grass swiftly but moves the clouds slowly, sometimes letting the sunlight touch the grass in small patches making random shapes and sometimes not letting the light reach the ground and the people. It has become slightly colder but not too cold, perfect for people to sit on the bench and just keep sitting, admiring everything around. It is hard to believe that the weather was so cruel to the children playing a while ago. It seems as if the sun, the clouds, the wind, the grass, the trees, the leaves, and the flowers have deliberately set it up, the moment they met.

After sitting there for more than they expected, they get up and leave for the market. *It is surprisingly tough to buy just some notebooks when you are with the person you are in love with,* he thinks. She gets some pens of all the colours Shivansh can name and more. Now the only thing left to buy was vegetables, the market for those is at the other end which means they can walk there and spend some more time. Together. On the way, Shivansh gets to see an ice cream shop. There's nothing edible in this world he loves more than ice cream.

'Why don't we have some ice cream before we go,' says Shivansh. Shweta couldn't unsee the spark in his eyes she had seen for the first time, *He was not this excited even when he won the match just now, just look at him now! What is it with this boy?*

'My treat!' she says with a wide smile and squinting eyes.

'Why…?'

'Why not?'

'Okay, but it's on me next time.'

'Sure.'

They reach in front of the counter and Shivansh asks for one black currant and one Belgium chocolate. Shweta looks at him but doesn't say anything, *he could've at least asked me. I mean I know I don't like anything in particular but… he could've asked me.* Shivansh knows that she neither has a favourite flavour nor does she want to try anything new on her own. He thinks she's cool with him ordering for her without asking her choice. They take the bench next to the shop.

Shivansh has everything he wants to buy and so does Shweta. Time flew by too fast for either of them to notice and it was already 6 pm. Since Shivansh lives far from this area, he should head back before it is too late. They start heading back to the ground where Shivansh secured an unassuming victory. Shivansh isn't too happy to leave so early, *we didn't even get to talk properly. Again.* Thinks Shivansh after spending three hours with her and that is exactly how she feels too. They can't think of anything else to talk about anymore.

'You are coming to school tomorrow, aren't you?' *Great! Why won't she come to school tomorrow, Shivansh? Can you give one simple reason for her not to? You should have stayed quiet, but you had to go the extra mile to say something stupid, didn't you? Damn! Why can't I think rationally in front of her?*

'Yes, why won't I?'

Exactly Shivansh! Why won't she? 'You don't seem the type to attend school daily...'

'I never miss school!' she pushes him with her elbow.

'Okay, I believe you.' *Right, she used to bunk the college, not the school. Now that I think about it, I don't think she ever missed school for no reason.*

They are now at an intersection; the bus stand is in the opposite direction to Shweta's house. Shweta looks at him before they go their separate ways, but Shivansh keeps walking without looking at her.

'Shivansh?' she says.

'What?'

'Don't you have to go that way?'

'Yes, but don't you live this way? Let me walk you home.'

'You know where I live?' she asks squinting her eyes.

'No…' *Shit! She hasn't shown me her house yet. How can I come out of this? Think Shivansh, fast, the longer you stay quiet the weirder it gets.* 'I don't think there are any residential buildings towards the bus stop and if we keep going straight then there's that convent school so, the only path that can lead us to your home is this one. Am I right?'

'Yeah…' she replies in awe. 'But you don't have to do this, I can go by myself.'

'I never said you can't. I'm coming with you because I'm a gentleman and it won't hurt to have your company for a little longer.' *Barely dodged this time! Shivansh, you have to be more careful with your words, you can't just spill anything you know without thinking about it twice.*

'Okay...' she doesn't know what else to say.

Shivansh wants to say something, anything, but he can't come up with anything. His heart is racing, faster than it did while playing. There is no one on the street but them, the red sky with the setting sun makes it hard to notice the slight blush on their faces. He is looking away from her, pretending to observe the surroundings and she is looking at her feet.

'Here we are...' Shweta sighs.

Shivansh turns his head to see her face, she's facing him but not looking at him. Before he can say something, she rings the bell.

'Mumma! I'm home.'

'Okay then, see tomorrow then' says Shivansh and turns back.

'Wait! Where are you going? Come in.'

'You know I'm already getting late, if I wait any longer, I might miss the last bus.'

'Yeah… at least have some water, you have been out since the morning.'

Her mother opens the door.

'Mumma, this is Shivansh, my classmate.'

'Namaste aunty ji!' Shivansh joins his hands to greet her mother.

'Namaste beta, come in, have something to eat.'

'Actually, I'm getting late.' says Shivansh.

'He doesn't live here; his house is near my school.' Shweta tells her.

'Just come in for a while if it gets too late your uncle will drop you back home, okay?'

'Aunty I'll come next time; I don't want to get scolded tonight.' He laughs a little.

'You have to come next time then, come and have a glass of water.'

Shivansh removes his shoes; Shweta and her mother ask him not to, but he does it anyway and enters. Shweta hurries and brings a glass of water for him, carrying a water bottle along in case he wants more. He gulps down the whole glass in one go and gets up to ask for permission to leave.

'If you don't come here next time…'

'I'll come for sure, thank you, Aunty Ji. Good night.'

Shivansh and Shweta get out of the house.

'You got everything you wanted, right?' asks Shivansh.

'Yeah.'

'Just to be sure, check your bag once you go back.'

'I said I got everything.'

'Please, just have a look. Especially, the smallest pocket.'

She gets flustered and asks, 'What did you do?'

'Nothing…' he smirks. 'Shweta, I gotta go now, Good night, sweet dreams.'

Shivansh turns back and starts walking. Shweta says nothing, she keeps standing at the door until she can no longer see him. She turns back and closes the door, 'Good night, Shivansh.'

CHAPTER 05: THE FAREWELL

This morning, Shivansh wakes up on time. Feeling refreshed after many days since he slept well. On the other edge of the city, Shweta is struggling just to open her eyes to look at the time like she's used to. After making the effort she manages to leave the bed, a smile pops up on her face when she remembers that she has yet to eat the chocolate he sneaked in her bag.

They both arrive at school on time, the day starts well for both of them. Shivansh realizes that he's able to focus in class despite waiting for a chance to strike up a conversation with her, see her face, look at her small hands move in a quirky way, getting blinded by the brightest smile on the planet, and lose himself in her entrancing eyes.

Mrs Rekha, the class teacher, enters the class. Like every other day, her lecture is the most fun and engaging but at the end of it, she announces that this is her last day at school, at least for a couple of months. She will be going on maternity leave. She's everyone's favourite, the class falls silent and not even a single student is not sad.

Shivansh, almost knowing what she is going to say asks, 'Ma'am, will you come to school tomorrow or…?'

'Yes, I need to be here tomorrow, but I shall not be taking any classes. I think I'll leave around lunchtime. And I'll make sure to see you all before leaving.'

The moment she leaves Shraddha goes in the front and says, 'Why don't we give her a nice present?' Almost everyone started giving their best ideas. She starts making a list on the blackboard to narrow down the ideas and decide on the best one. In the end, it comes down to the person who will go to the shop and buy the gift.

'I'll buy it this evening, but I want someone to come with me in case the gift we want is not available, we can decide on something else then and there.' Says Shivansh.

None of the boys show interest, just the way Shivansh thought. Shraddha jumps in again to help him, 'I'm going to the market with my mom so, I don't think I'll be able to manage enough time. Shweta, would you go with him? I can't trust boys on this one anyway.'

Shweta agrees and it is decided that they will be going to buy the gift. Both find it hard to hide their smile and pretend that nothing is out of the ordinary.

After school, they decide to go to the nearest gift shop, but Shivansh is hungry and so is Shweta. It just makes everything harder and more frustrating; having an argument with her is the last thing Shivansh wants to do with her today, or ever. They roam in the shop in silence, trying to find the one thing they have come for. Minutes pass but they still haven't found the gift and the cherry on top was a scent making their mouth watery.

'I think something delicious is being prepared in the *Dhaba*, it's just right next to this shop. Why don't we grab a bite first? You hungry? I definitely am.' says Shivansh.

'Yeah sure, I was just waiting for you to ask actually.'

'Typical you…'

'What?' Shweta is confused about what he means by that.

Shivansh! Just how many times are you going to do this?

'Kidding! Ha ha ha... Let's go I'm starving!'

He opens the gate for her and says, 'After you.' Shweta cannot tell if he's being a gentleman or if he's trying to pull a prank of some sort. Being fellow introverts they both lock their eyes on a table in the corner, it is empty. Sitting, they wait for someone to bring the menu. Shivansh sits comfortably and pours some water for her. She looks left and right and takes the glass from Shivansh's hand.

'So, did you get *The Fault in Our Stars*?'

'Not yet, but I'm planning to get it soon.'

'You'll love it,' he says in a high-spirited voice.

'How'd you know?' she squints her eyes.

'I just know...' *I mean how can I not know?*

A young boy interrupts and offers them the menu. Shivansh takes the menu and looks at Shweta, asking if there is something she would like to get but she replies the way he knew she would, 'I'll just have the same as you.'

'Two plates of *Rajma Chawal* please.'

Shweta's eyes pop out in surprise, 'You like *Rajma Chawal* too?' she says in the loudest voice Shivansh has heard since they met in this life.

'What happened? Is this your favourite dish or something?' he says knowing the obvious answer.

'You bet it is! You didn't tell, do you like it?'

'I'm sure I don't love it the way you do. It's okay, I guess.'

'Then why'd you order it?'

'Just felt like eating *Rajma Chawal* today...'

'So, do you have any idea for the gift? I don't think they have what we want.'

'I think I do have something in mind.'

'What is it?'

'You'll know once you see it.'

Two plates of a dish that Shweta loves, and Shivansh doesn't like, arrive at the table with two chilled glasses of buttermilk. Shivansh watches Shweta as she eats and talks, her hair slides in front of her face making it harder for her to enjoy her favourite meal, she tucks it in the back of her ear the way Shivansh wants to do it for her but controls himself with his peak willpower. He loves the way she eats so gracefully; she eats slowly but with peace.

Both have their tummies filled and now they can concentrate on the gift. After getting back to the shop, Shweta waits as Shivansh looks for the thing he has in his mind. *It was around here I think, c'mon it's been ten years. Keep looking Shivansh, you know it is here.* He keeps moving the decorative items to look behind them and finally, it is there. The same place where he found it in his past. A figurine of a baby with small wings similar to that of an angel, it is not a Cupid though. He takes it out and shows it to her.

'Woah! It's so cute. I think it's perfect.'

'Let's get it then.' He asks the shopkeeper to gift-wrap it. They both come out of the shop with faces lit up with smiles.

'Do you want to get anything else?'

'Umm, I don't know. I think I don't need anything right now.'

'I didn't ask if you needed anything, I asked if you wanted something' he smirks.

'I know and I don't want anything' She pushes her elbow into his stomach.

'Careful! I'm full, you don't want everything spilling out, do you?'

They both laugh. Shivansh takes her to the bus stop; they continue to laugh on their way and are now silent. Shweta sits where she usually does and Shivansh stands outside. Nothing more to say to each other they just look at each other till the bus starts to move.

'Did you check your bag?' Shivansh shouts.

'Oh god! Again?' She quickly checks her bag, and finds a chocolate, just like last time. *How does he do that? This has happened twice, and I not only failed to notice when he sneaked one in my bag but also when he even bought a chocolate when I was around. Does he always carry one with him or what?* She waves at him with a bright smile and that alone makes it all worthwhile for him.

The next morning, they tell how they couldn't find anything on the list and finally got a perfect gift for Mrs Rekha. Shraddha tells the same to the class. The whole class is waiting for her to come before she leaves. She comes the moment lunch break starts; she gives her blessings to the class. Today, no one has even opened their lunch boxes, all are busy talking and listening to Mrs Rekha. Most of the girls have started crying, the boys are making fun of them, and they are sad to see Mrs. Rekha leave.

Just when Rekha is about to leave, Shraddha, Shweta, and Shivansh come closer to her. Shraddha hands her the present, 'Ma'am, this is from everyone in the class.' She cannot believe her eyes; her little kid students have bought her a parting gift. She gets teary-eyed. Unwraps the gift, nobody in the class knows what's inside that except Shivansh and Shweta. The "winged baby" makes his first appearance in front of everyone. 'Awwwwww' says most of the girls in the class. There is hardly anyone who can say that there can be a better gift than this one.

'Thank you, everyone, I thank you all from the bottom of my heart for such a cute gift. Believe me, it is more than enough that you all went out of your way to get me something but this, this is the cutest gift I have ever received. I'll keep it in a place where I can see it every day, it'll keep reminding me about all of you. I am so happy. I'll miss you all. Keep working diligently and do good in your exams.' She leaves.

Her absence made the class quiet, so quiet that even Mr Ram is shocked that he doesn't have to yell at the class. He decides to ignore this peculiar behaviour and starts writing about today's topic. As he leaves the class, he wonders why he didn't have to ask the class to keep it silent even once.

Today, all the remaining periods were the same, silent. Just like Mr. Ram, every teacher finds it hard to believe that this class is not making any noise. The bell announces the end of the day, and everyone takes their bag and drags their feet as they leave for their homes. Shivansh and Shweta manage to share a glance, they both know this is all the time they get today with each other and now they can only wait for the next day to come.

Tonight, Shivansh stares at the ceiling. Thinking about the way his new life's been taking shape. Everything is going unbelievably smoothly which makes him a little worried. *Life can never be kind, either I'm a genius or something is going to get really ugly. Maybe, something already went wrong, and I just haven't noticed it yet. This can be worse; I need to cross-check everything. I cannot shake this feeling that happens when everything goes nicely for a couple of days, something is bound to happen to balance it out. There is a chance that I'm just overthinking and everything is normal, and just thinking about it won't do any good. For now, I think I should just stop thinking and relax, it's not good for a schoolboy to take so much on his shoulders.*

I wonder what Shweta is doing, the one this whole fuss is about, this whole new life is about. I bet she's buried under tonnes of blankets and still feeling a little cold and cursing the weather of Nainital. He then imagines just how cute her face would look in the moonlight coming through her window when she wakes up with her eyes closed and struggling to find the water bottle beside her bed. How she would…—he falls asleep, thinking about her.

"Such a great day!" she writes today's last line in her journal. *I can't believe I had such a great day on a school day. I will miss Rekha ma'am. I knew she would love the present; it was so cute after all. It was fun finding and buying that. It's always fun with him. I was really shocked to see him ordering Rajma Chawal. I don't know how he pulls stuff like this, but he always manages to do something crazy yet somehow familiar. I don't know why I feel like he knows me, better than the rest of my friends, it feels like he understands me. It feels so easy to talk to him, I don't have to think when I talk to him. Most of the fun I had today was thanks to him, but I didn't even get to tell him that. Can I even say something like that? What will he think if I say so?*

Anyway, I just hope that days like this continue to come frequently, where I can have fun, and a little adventure time with him, and in the end, I can easily say that it was a great day. It was time for her to sleep but unlike most of the days, sleep isn't kind to her today too. Nothing else to do she grabs a book and starts reading. *A book can do wonders, it can make you a great personality and it can also help you fall asleep.* She laughs to herself. She starts to see the wonder her book is doing; it's making her eyes feel heavier and hard to keep open. She puts the book on the side table with a cute girly bookmark in it, takes a sip of warm water pulls the third blanket over her face, and closes her eyes to fall asleep.

CHAPTER 06: THE SECRET SUNSET POINT

The month of August is about to pass. The windy and perfectly cool weather slowly turns into an always-too-cold to bear. About a fortnight passed since Shivansh saw Shweta for the first time in his life.

He is now wholly settled living as a teenager again, he has felt unbound gratitude for what he has been provided with since the day he woke up, getting to live with his parents, eat his mother's handmade cooking, quarrel with his little brother and even getting to see her again, there is nothing he can ask for more.

It is the sports period; the boys are playing football. The sun radiates its finely controlled heat to the young boys, there is no wind, making the weather ideal for playing. All the boys running wildly are suddenly stopped by a whistle which they think is to indicate the time to get back to their classrooms but to everyone's surprise, the coach announces a friendly match with another school.

'We are going to Haldwani to play a friendly football match at the end of September. Those who want to participate will come to me and I'll tell you how we are going, when we are going, how many are going, and everything else there. Start practising now if you want to get selected.' He says and leaves.

How can I forget about this? He thinks. *I have played this match in the past and I remember that we lost brutally. Now, however, I really want to win this time but just knowing how and what is going to happen doesn't make me omnipotent. I just can't defeat a team like theirs with only knowledge of the past.*

I know why we lost, we were not playing as a team but with some individuals, all trying to trap the ball and score. We had no coordination, we barely passed the ball around and the worst thing was that we had no formation, almost all of us kept running for the ball wherever it went, and they made us dance like idiots. I will turn things around this time. I need to build a team from scratch, and I should do this now.

Shivansh calls everyone and starts discussing the game. As expected, everyone wanted to play but not to win, most of them just wanted to have a nice tour from school. Seeing Shivansh so fired up, some fire sparked in them too. They are starting to think differently, in a better way, they can enjoy the tour, but they can enjoy it harder if they come back as winners. Shivansh finishes the little talk, covering everything including a rough practising routine for the next few days which he will later update with some research.

Without any delay, everybody started practising the drills Shivansh suggested earlier. They have many problems to deal with, they don't have a football coach. Being a small school, having a little over 300 students, they have only one PE teacher. Pramod was once a national-level champion in taekwondo, he even played some international matches and now coaches young students at Kendriya Vidyalaya, Nainital. Despite being a specialist in one sport, he has basic knowledge of almost all other common games. Generally, he manages all the sports activities and tournaments.

Lunch break is over now; everyone goes back to their classes, but Shivansh goes to Mr Pramod to talk about the match. He tells Shivansh everything he needs to know. A total of 18 players will be selected to play against St. Xavier's School, Haldwani. The team will depart on the 30th of September at 5 in the morning, reaching there by 7-7:30 and having breakfast then some rest. The match will start at 11. After lunch, some leisure time will be given to the players. At 6:30 the team will leave from there and by 9 o'clock in the night all will be back here.

Shivansh remembers how good the Haldwanians were, his team was one-sidedly beaten by them with a score of 4-0. It's been a very long time since he played the match, but he remembers it in pieces and the last thing he wants is to lose the game a second time. With the bits and pieces, he can collect from his memory, he tries to come up with ways to build a team good enough to beat them.

Everyone interested in playing the match kept practising daily for two weeks. All the practice matches and drills are suggested and looked over by Shivansh himself. Having the experience of a 26-year-old dude certainly proves helpful in situations like these.

September 21, Shivansh is selected as the team captain. With the selection completed and the team selected, he now has fewer players to give time to so, he can practice even more. Everything is going well enough for him and all he can see is victory coming to him. The team has been practising a lot, perfecting their positioning and passes, which was their biggest weakness and arguably the major cause of their defeat last time, since day one. Shivansh did not even once tell anyone verbally to pass or not leave their position, he focused solely on drills and practice matches. Most of the players observed that drills that they have been doing are actually practical and helpful, and positioning does work wonders while playing an actual match.

Good thing I looked up all those drills on the internet. I could only remember a few of them but now I can see us winning against them, not easily but there are chances of us winning, Shivansh thinks with a smile on his face when he watches his team play, like a team.

The match is right after next week and after having gone through such challenging practice, the team's confidence is sky-high. Everyone, in adShraddhaon to being in high spirits, seems fully prepared for the match.

Now that Shivansh feels a little assured about it too, he can now manage to think about other things. So many days have passed without him getting to talk to Shweta properly for once, they have only been able to chat for a while in class but that was nowhere close to what they wanted.

The match is on Monday, making it easier to have time to meet with her before the match and he does find a way. They will have a light practice on Sunday morning and then complete rest till the match, since he will be free after that he can meet her right after the match like last time. All that is left is to ask her and he can feel that she is going to say yes.

He again waits till the school is over and then as everyone starts to move, he goes and stands near her bus which he loves to do every now and then, especially when they don't get enough time to talk in school. Shweta, unaware of him, goes inside the bus and takes her regular seat, only to find him standing right by her window.

'Check your bag' he shouts.

Shweta rolls her eyes, 'Not again!' She finds another piece of chocolate with a small note in her bag. In it, he has written about the practice on Saturday and a question.

> I know you know that on the 30th I'm going to Haldwani for a football match. So, on Sunday, we have decided to have a light exercise in the morning and after that, we are basically free. I'll be leaving on a Monday morning and will be back by dinner time. So, I was wondering if you have anything planned this Sunday or not. If not, I think we can then have another round of shopping since my notebook which I bought last time is lost so, I really need a new one. Do come if you have time.
>
> -Shivansh

She gives her "yes" by nodding her head with a big smile on her face. Her cheeks look bright pink. Shivansh finds himself lost in awe; she looks just like "*Munni*" from "Bajrangi Bhaijaan" while nodding, a Bollywood film yet to be released. He cannot be happier than he is right now, his team looks prepared and the girl he loves agrees to meet him, what more can he even ask for right now? *The joy of being a kid.*

He reaches home in a hurry; he wants to revise some of his syllabus. For the past few days, he was busy practising and couldn't make time for his studies. He doesn't want to score badly and get all his freedom taken away from him.

'You are smiling all the time these days,' says Pooja as she opens the door.

'What do you mean?' says Shivansh as he enters, hiding his face from her.

'C'mon, you can tell me, I'm your mother.'

'There is nothing to TELL, Maa'

'Okay, my son is all grown up. Having secrets from his own mother.'

'Seriously Maa? I'm telling you there is nothing. And I'm really hungry, and I have to study after that. Please tell me there is something to eat.'

'Yes, there is. You go and freshen up first.'

Shivansh starts to study right after lunch and goes to play in the evening. Comes back and again studies till dinner time. Finishes up all the chores and gets in bed early. Tomorrow being Sunday means practice in the morning and then getting to spend some time with her. To perform well enough in practice, his body needs rest which he cannot compromise on.

A week passed and it was Sunday again, September 29. The weather is colder than it was on the last week, and it gets harder for him to get up early in the morning. He finds himself alone on the ground when most people are sleeping in their cosy beds on a Sunday morning as good as this. There is some fog so it's hard to see too far. He takes a look at his watch; *I think I'll have to wait for at least an hour for everyone else.*

The sky and the clouds are painted in a slight tint of pink, the kind of pink that makes you want to sit and keep watching. Tiny droplets of water covered the grass across the ground. Breeze keeps hinting that the winter is coming. Shivansh keeps his hands in his side pockets. Shivansh had planned to start warming up the moment he reached the ground but now he is just sitting and admiring the place he is in.

One man makes himself visible from a distance from the fog, then another, and one more, they are jogging. *Quite the health-conscious people they are.* He decides to get up and walk around and across the fog. He starts walking and the wind hits his face harder, the people he saw jogging went in the other direction. Someone else is there besides the four of them. That person is sitting on the bench, Shivansh gets closer and closer as he continues to walk. It's her. She's wearing a cute maroon woollen cap and several layers of clothing of the same colour family. She's even wearing gloves that have a childish kitten design on them, maybe it's hard to find better designs if someone has hands this small. The closer he gets the easier it becomes to see her face, puffy cheeks, and small nose glowing like a tomato.

'Why are you here this early in the morning?' asks Shivansh, pleasantly surprised.

'I had nothing to do.' Shivansh sits beside her, and he notices that he can see the world in her eyes and it looks prettier than what he's been looking at since the last five minutes. For a while, they both sit in silence. Awkward yet somehow peaceful at the same time. Trying to defeat the silence, Shivansh says. 'What do you like to do in your free time?'

'I don't do much, I study most of the time and I read other books and novels. I'm not an outdoor person so, I don't play outside as much.'

'You are boring! You read books other than the books we have to read at school! I mean, why? Just why? I hate books!'

'Yes, I am,' she retorts.

'No, you are not. I am just joking. You are very interesting. And cool. And nice.' *And beautiful, pretty, cute, loving, caring, adorable, thoughtful, graceful, comforting, enchanting, inspiring, sensitive, pure...*

'I don't know what to say to that,' she brings him back from the train of his thoughts.

'You don't need to, I get it' *I get YOU.* 'Just remember you are not boring, not even close.'

'Look, your friends are here. How long are you going to make me wait this time?' she points to some boys entering the ground with her tiny index finger, the way Shivansh loves. Fog starts to lift, early morning sun rays deliver a comforting warmth to the surroundings, and small drops of water from grass and tree leaves start to evaporate mixing a heavenly aroma all around.

'I don't want to make you wait but you came before even the practice starts...' he makes a sad face.

'I know, I know, I'm kidding. Just go and have a blast.' she interrupts.

Practice starts as the last one arrives; they start with a warm-up routine. Shivansh tries hard to keep his focus on the practice. After nearly two hours of moderate drills, Shivansh gathers everyone and gives a short talk. He asks everyone to have complete rest till the match and no one will come to play this evening. Everyone then goes their separate ways; Shivansh goes to Shweta.

'So, what do we do now?' hoping Shweta will say something that she likes to do.

'First, sit here for a while Mr. *I'm not tired'* she mimics him again.

'Sure!' Shivansh bursts into laughter, *I just cannot handle this much cuteness!* Grabs the water bottle from her, just like last time. *She's so caring, I love her!*

'Do you have anything to get done today?' he says after gulping down some big sips.

'Nothing, I just told you I don't have anything to do today.'

'Yeah, you did but seriously, you don't have anything in mind?'

'Seriously, I don't. You tell me what to do, and where to go, I am totally free. I just need to get back home before it gets dark, that's it.'

'Did your mom say so?' Shivansh asks. 'Maa says the exact same words every day! "Get home before it gets dark."'

'Yeah, moms...'

'Tell me about your mom apart from her being so pretty.'

'She's just amazing, I tell her everything.'

'That's great, you know you look like her a lot, right?'

'Yeah, people tell me so...'

'Let's go now, I think I remember a place we can visit.'

'Where to?' she raises her eyebrows.

'Don't ask, just come with me. And I don't want you to get late so, hurry.'

'Shut up' She gets up and tries to hang her bag on her shoulders.

'Now you know what to say.' Shivansh chuckles and takes her bag from her; she hesitates but gives up in the end. She has no idea where he is going to take her, but it makes her think more about Shivansh, *what is he planning? Why does it always feel like he knows about me, like he knows me? We must be going somewhere far, he said he doesn't want me to get late. Who says that? He could've just said that he doesn't want to get late.* Many thoughts keep popping in her head and with time they are close to the place where Shivansh is taking her.

She is tired. She bends and holds her knees, 'How...'

'We are here just a little more, come.' He replies before she can complete it.

'Yes, coming.' She rolls her eyes and starts walking again.

'This is the sunset point!' says Shivansh taking a seat on a cement block at the edge of the road.

'This is not. Don't tell me you wanted to go the sunset point but got lost.'

'Yes, it's not the sunset point everyone knows. It's the one that I found, it's mine and now yours too.'

Shweta doesn't respond to this; she has no words. She follows him, and he carefully goes down the slope and helps her to get down as well. Within a few steps, they reach a place where they can sit and have a clear view of sunset in silence.

'This place is so quiet,' she says as she sits on the ground.

'I know right, and that sunset point is always crowded. Nobody knows about this place it is always like this. You won't hear a thing here, not even vehicle noises. It is worth watching a sunset in silence, isn't it?'

'Yes, it is but don't you think we arrived a little too soon to watch sunset? It's not even noon yet.'

'That's exactly what I was thinking.'

They laugh a little and keep talking until they get hungry; Shivansh goes to get some food for both of them. Shweta waits for him and then they both enjoy the meal under a tree. After having lunch, they both lie down and continue talking.

'Shweta! Wake up. Look!' Shivansh finds out that they have been sleeping for two hours and it is almost time for sunset, *Glad that we didn't miss the sunset.*

Shweta gets up and rubs her eyes with the back of her hands. As soon as her head gets clearer and she's completely awake, she feels a little embarrassed. Shivansh notices that and tells her that they both fell asleep.

'But the good part is we haven't missed the sunset.'

They both sit, looking at the sun. The sun is now bigger but less bright than it was in the day. This peach colour that the sun is dyed in, leaks into the sky and dyes the clouds too. They both sit in silence and let everything sink in. The wind starts to get stronger, it flows through the sharp leaves of pine trees and makes noise, noise that feels good to the ears. It has a certain peace to it. It is getting colder but both of them have their eyes locked on the sun. The surroundings become quieter; the birds have stopped their singing. They are afraid of the dark, getting back to their homes before the sun sets completely. The sun touches the horizon.

'So, what do you think?' Shivansh asks without moving his head.

'It's beautiful,' she can't say more, there's no need to, looking at the sun.

They keep looking till the time the sun hides behind the horizon. Shweta wants to stay, and so does Shivansh.

'I think we should head back,' says Shivansh in a low voice.

Shweta just nods and starts to follow him. He climbs up on the same path to get to the road and grabs her hand to pull her up. They don't have much time before it gets dark. Shivansh drops Shweta at her house and leaves, *good thing Aunty didn't see me today.*

Shivansh gets home late, later than usual and gets a good amount of lecture from his mother. *Was it worth it? Yes, definitely yes!* It worked in his favour in every way possible. He had such a nice time with Shweta and after getting scolded like that he realised that he missed it, the scolding he used to get from his Maa. *I cannot remember when the last time she scolded me like this.* He doesn't even try to make any excuses, he just keeps standing and receives all her mother's love in the form of scolding. It eventually ends as a mother's heart melts too quickly. She tries her best to sound angry and asks him to bathe and sit with his mouth shut, dinner is almost ready.

It is dinner time; everyone sits on the carpet with their legs crossed. Shivansh surprisingly finishes first and waits for everyone else. Greets good night and goes to bed. Looking at the ceiling he thinks about his day, the time he spent with her. *No, now is not the time to think about her.* He forces his thoughts to shift towards the match the next day and falls asleep.

The awaited day finally arrives, perfect weather to have a match. It's five in the morning and 18 students with Mr. Pramod leave for Haldwani while the rest of the students aren't even awake. By the time they reach the school, their football team will be standing in St. Xavier's School. Coach tells them all the Do's and Don'ts along the way. The journey feels unreal, the bus takes sharp turns frequently and bottomless valleys can be seen right outside the road. It's still dark but some light makes way to everything right before the sunrise. Some of them start singing random songs. Shivansh, clearly, is not interested in that. He keeps looking out the window, he feels nostalgic as he remembers the path, the noise in the bus, the view, valleys, the wind hitting his face, the clouds running along with him, barely visible moon. Aakash screams, 'We are here,' in Shivansh's ear, point blank. He jumps out and pulls his ear real hard.

'Sorry, sorry, let's go now!' says Aakash trying to get away from him.

'Yeah, let's go. You better play well today. Don't keep daydreaming about Shraddha during the match.' Pinches his ear harder for one last time before he lets him go.

'What are you talking about?' says Aakash as he looks away from him.

'I can't tell if you don't tell me. Let's get off the bus now, we are last.' He smirks.

'Okay...' still looking away from him.

They go outside and see everyone waiting for them, they run and join the line. Pramod doesn't want to give a scolding right before the match, so he lets it slide. He takes them to the canteen for breakfast.

An empty room is given to them for resting and changing by the school. Some are talking, some are sleeping, and the rest are talking to their parents through cell phones.

10:15 a.m., Pramod takes the team to the ground for stretching and warm-up.

11:00 a.m., Both teams are ready, and players have taken their positions. Captains go to the referee for the toss. Shivansh, as usual, loses the toss. Rahul, team Haldwani's captain, chooses to kick off. Shivansh is left to choose the half.

Shivansh realises that Rahul made a mistake choosing to kick off right away, he should have noticed the weather, it is perfect to take advantage of, with strong winds from the east and the sun acting all high and mighty. He chooses the east half. For the next 45 minutes, Haldwanians are going to face the sun and strong wind against them, this will tire them out.

The match starts with Haldwanians kicking off the ball. Showing the talent and teamwork Shivansh still remembers, they take the ball near the goal post within the first 5 minutes despite the disadvantages. It is the first time for KVians to face a team like this one, they lose patience quickly and break their formation running behind the ball. Shivansh shouts and reorganises the formation, after struggling for a couple of minutes KVians get hold of the ball. This calms everyone in Shivansh's team, they continue to slowly approach the opponents' half connecting numerous passes.

Possession of the ball changes again and again in the first half and no matter how dominating the Haldwanians are, the score remains 0-0.

Half time, both teams feel a little tired, sit and drink some juice and discuss their strategy for the second half.

Shivansh found a way to score a goal and if lucky then maybe even more.

'We all know that this team is a little too good for us,' he takes a pause, 'But I know how to win this. If you are with me then I think we can go home with a trophy.'

He tells the team a step-by-step plan to follow blindly and trusts him to score. After seeing him build up the team the way he did and holding their ground only after practising for a month, they cannot help but trust him with this game. With everyone on the same page as him,

Shivansh steps back in the ground intending to switch from playing defensive to wild offence.

Pramod tries his best to cheer up the boys with some cliché lines like, "Participating is more important than winning" but he then realises that the boys are not here to lose gracefully but to win, at any cost.

The whistle gets blown; the players again take their positions but on different halves. Shivansh starts with the kick-off, and KVians keep passing the ball without any intention to score the goal. Haldwanians keep chasing the ball and to their surprise, it is now much harder to steal the ball from than it was in the first half. They can't tell what they are thinking but it is clear that they do have something in mind.

Haldwanians are growing restless, just the way Shivansh has planned. His classic tactic works almost all the time, especially with teenagers. He keeps the same flow for 15 minutes and by the time Haldwanians lose their guard, KVians attack. Two players remain in their half and the rest charge towards the goalpost all at once, throwing them into chaos. Haldwanians cannot grasp what their amateur opponents are trying to do, they try to defend but they are coming at them quickly, faster than they expected. With the sudden rush, Shivansh catches them unprepared and receives a header right next to the goalpost, score! 1-0.

KVians manage to score their first goal, Shivansh runs back to his team, they cheer for the goal and on the whistle get back to their positions. Shivansh can feel his heart beating louder than ever, only 15 minutes are left, if they manage to maintain the lead, they win. To Shivansh's surprise, his team doesn't slow down after their first goal, they charge at Haldwanians for the possession of the ball. Several minutes have passed and KVians get the ball back, they again start by slowly pressing on them with nonstop passes. They again press hard for a goal but the whistle blows, ending the match. Final score: (Kendriya Vidyalaya, Nainital) 1: (St. Xavier's School, Haldwani) 0.

9:12 p.m., Shivansh arrives home with the trophy, only for one night. He can only hope to see Shweta the next day. He will bring the trophy to school after all, the trophy will be displayed in the school hall. Pooja takes his medal and certificate, she will later hang the medal on the living room wall and keep the certificate in a folder, where all his certificates are.

I can't wait! He must be back by now, but I don't know if he won the match. Ugh! This is so frustrating. Shweta struggles to sleep, waiting for the next day to see him and ask him about the match.

October 1st, Shivansh walks to school with his chest out. Holding a trophy does attract attention, everyone looks at him. He reaches his class shows everyone the trophy and receives tonnes of compliments; Shweta looks at him while still sitting on her bench. She has no idea how to react, or what to say to him. Shivansh reads her eyes and gives her a nod, telling her that it's all right, she doesn't have to say anything. As everybody starts to move to the assembly ground, Shivansh hands the trophy to Aakash to avoid the attention he's been getting since the moment he entered the school. He walks slowly, slower than everyone else and joins Shweta.

'Congratulations!' she says almost too loud.

'Thank you.' Silence. Before he can think of something to say, they reach the assembly ground.

After the prayer, the football team is called upon the stage. One by one Mrs Pushpa honours the 18 players with medals and a photo is about to get clicked with the whole team.

Shivansh finds the eyes he wanted to look at him, only him. Shweta looks at him and claps in high spirits, she looks so happy. One can easily notice the redness in her cheeks from the excitement and smiling so hard.

Seeing Shweta like this, his heart leaps up in happiness. The photo is clicked, he smiles so hard his eyes get closed and the same redness can now be seen on his cheeks as well. *This is only going to get better. I wish this never ends.*

In class, Shivansh finds everyone coming to him and congratulating him on the victory, but his eyes only wait for her. *I can't even imagine how she will talk to me; she was so excited in the assembly. Seeing her happy is such bliss. I can't get enough of it, not in this life.* She comes. His heart beats faster. *What is happening? I've talking to her for so long, why am I feeling like this? What do you even say about a feeling like this? She is not going to confess Shivansh, stay calm! It's all right. Everything is under control.*

'Hey Shivansh, congratulations!' she says with a smile that melts his heart, this is the second time she has congratulated him but he is still too happy to say something.

'...' he stays silent, just looks at her.

'What?'

'Nothing just... Thank you. I wish you could have seen me, and others play. I think we played quite well.' *Just thinking about her cheering for me, I could have scored another goal or two.* 'You say, what did you do? What happened here at school?'

'Yeah, it could have been great if we all saw our team play and win. Nothing really happened here, just the usual.'

'So, did you miss me?' he whispers leaning closer to her.

Her face turns red in a second and she gets up and goes back to her seat. *Did I say too much? Shit! Is she angry? Will she talk to me? Why? Why did I say that? It was going so well, and I ruined it, I always ruin it. I ruined it last time too, and she never came back. If I didn't get this chance, if this miracle hadn't happened, I would have lived the rest of my life without her.* Countless thoughts numb Shivansh's body, he doesn't know what to do. He's been looking at her since she left, and she turns back and looks at him. Her face glows red, even brighter than it glowed earlier, and she nods. All of a sudden, all the thoughts in his head get quiet. *Did she just say yes? Yes, she did! I didn't mess up this time. Nothing is collapsing, it'll be all right. I'll live with her forever, if not in my previous life, then in this life. I will not mess it up this time.*

CHAPTER 07: GETTING CLOSER

Not many days have passed since the match against the Haldwanians, and there comes another sports event on the roaster. This time, it's a school-level table tennis competition. Last time, Shivansh had no idea about it but this time, he is ready, he knows Shraddha will eventually come to him and drag him out to play. She is in the same house as him, Tagore house. Not so great for Shivansh, Shweta is in Raman house. *I wish we were in the same house...* he thinks.

As expected of Shraddha, like any other event, table tennis competition couldn't escape her radar. She comes running to Shivansh at lunchtime and tells him about the event. He has to act like this is the first time he has heard about this.

'Come with me.' She demands.

'What? Where?' Even knowing about everything isn't enough to not get surprised by her exceptionally high energy.

'There's an inter-house table tennis competition and you are going to participate in it.'

'Do I have to…?' he knows there's no way she won't let him stay out, still trying to tease her a little.

Her eyes widen, and she tries to raise one of her eyebrows, which she is incapable of, and goes, 'Yes, you have to!'

'Okay, but I have never played it before.'

'Don't worry, you can now.'

'Right now?'

'Yes!'

He finds himself in the same spot he was in 13 years ago. Pramod teaches him the basics, the rules, the way to hold the bat, everything. It took about 20 minutes to get familiar with the game when played it for the first time in his life but now just to see crazy expressions on everyone's face, he plays like a pro the moment he holds the bat.

'Seriously, this is your first time playing this game?' asks Pramod.

He can see the shock on Shraddha's face as well. *I'm sure she will ask unending questions when we'll head back. It did feel a little weird playing in this body, but I managed better than I had expected.* It is obvious enough that he is going to play for Tagore House and most of them even expected him to get the first position, but Pramod has to announce the playing members after they have seen everybody play.

'For Tagore House, Shivansh and Ravi will be playing for the boys' team and Shraddha will be playing for the girls' team.'

Ravi and Shraddha get really excited to hear their names, Shivansh behaves as though he knows that he is going to get selected, which is true as he did know everything after all.

I won when I actually played it for the first time and now, I'm literally overpowered in front of these kids. He smirks.

They go running to Shweta to tell her that they just got selected and to their surprise, she will be playing for her house. She does not want to, but the teachers didn't leave her with any other choice. Shivansh practised every evening with his friends last time but he doesn't need practice this time, so he offers to teach Shweta, Shraddha and Ravi.

'Shweta you won't believe just how good Shivansh is. I think he is going to win the tournament without breaking any sweat' says Shraddha, helping Shivansh to gain some plus points in her eyes. Ravi joins her, 'He really knows how to play, how long have you played Shivansh?'

'Seriously, this is my first time playing this game and I wouldn't even have tried to play if it weren't for Shraddha. She dragged me into this when I didn't even want to play but to tell you the truth I actually enjoyed playing, I guess I'm natural with it. So, what do you say? Let's practice daily in the evening till the tournament.'

'I'm definitely coming' says Shraddha.

'And so am I' says Ravi. All start to stare at Shweta with hope.

'Okay, okay, I'll join you guys. Just don't expect too much from me, please.'

Shivansh and Shraddha laugh. Ravi has no idea of what is going on.

'Can't we just play in the sports period?' says Shweta, trying to reduce the practice sessions.

'No, because one, it won't be enough and two, you won't get to play much because everyone will practice in the sports period.' Says Shivansh making the daily practice the last option. Sadly, luck is not on Shweta's side today.

'That's right but do you have any other great ideas, genius? Like where are we even going to play and how are we going to get the gear?' says Shraddha, coming for her friend's rescue.

'I do know a place where we can practice, and I can arrange all the necessary things too.'

'But…' says Shweta, expecting a catch in these readily available facilities.

'But the place is close to our houses, not yours Shweta, yes that's the only but' says Shivansh.

'How far is it?' she sounds determined.

'Well, if you can manage to come near the school then we'll just have to walk for 10 minutes.'

'I think I can manage that, I'll just have to catch the bus after practice back home, right?'

'Yeah, great then, see you both at the school gate at 4' says Shivansh.

'Today?' both Shweta and Shraddha say in a high pitch.

'We don't have much time guys, only two weeks. And do you have any other plans?'

'No, but... all right I'll be there' says Shraddha.

'Me too' says Ravi after staying quiet through the whole thing.

'I don't have anything else to do so yeah, I'll come too,' says Shweta.

With everything figured out, they go to practice in the little time they are left with.

In the evening, Shweta comes back to the school gate and sees Shivansh and Shraddha talking to each other. She feels uneasy, there is something that's irritating her, but she cannot point her finger at it. *Since when did they become friends? I thought they just knew each other.* What she feels is a little jealousy but she's not ready to accept that.

'Can we start the practice if you two are done?' she says, announcing just how annoyed she is.

'Yeah, we were just waiting for you,' says oblivious Shivansh with a broad smile, happy to see her again.

Shraddha can clearly see what's going on, Shweta is jealous as hell and Shivansh is as clueless as ever.

Shivansh leads the way and as they start walking, Shraddha takes the rear, allowing them to keep talking without any interruptions. He even asks them to jog to the place for a little warm-up, but Shweta couldn't disagree more. After a ten-minute walk, they all reach the place where they can practice for the victory. They go inside the building to a hall with a table in the centre. They spend some time tidying up the place, and Shivansh hands them the rackets.

'I could get only two'

'Well, only two can play at once. So, what's the issue' says Shraddha.

'Technically four but never mind, let's start'

Shweta and Shraddha start to play, while Shivansh coaches them. He tells them everything from how to hold the bat to how to smash, turns out it is too early to teach them the latter. He continues with the basics. After some time, not-so-athletic Shweta loses her breath. Shivansh enters the ring, *I cannot play seriously with her, she's new to the game, unlike someone who came back to the past.* He plays in a perfect balance between too easy and overpowering. Shraddha being the possessor of great intuitions can guess that Shivansh is playing with her in a way that is challenging enough to pull the best game out of her.

Seeing them play together, Shweta again feels that unsettling feeling she felt earlier, she's not as tired now but she hesitates to ask to play with him. Having Shivansh as her opponent, it was impossible for her not to play giving it her all.

'Shweta, I'm really tired, you want to switch?' she says.

'Sure!' Shweta jumps from the bench with a radiant smile.

Damn! That smile can make the whole Nainital go blind.

'I didn't know you liked table tennis this much,' Shraddha says with a smirk.

'I don't, I mean I am starting to like this game but not that much,' says Shweta trying her best to cover her excitement. She takes the bat from her and takes her spot.

'You ready? Or are you tired too?'

'Me? You'll have to work much harder to make me break a sweat' says Shivansh.

'Just you wait, once I learn to play this, I'll crush you.'

'Sure, looking forward to that day, if it ever comes.'

He wants to keep playing for as long as he can, so he just returns the ball to the other side easy enough for her to play. The rallies are way longer than they were with Shraddha. Seeing them play like this, with their happy faces, she knows exactly what to do. She gets up and says, 'I'll just come back in a moment' and leaves the hall. She is not surprised by the fact that neither of them replied to her, they aren't even aware that she is leaving.

Shraddha goes outside to take a breather; she takes out the glucon-D water her mom gave her and sips through half of it. She takes a seat and waits for them to come out eventually if they do think about her.

Shivansh and Shweta are still playing, still unaware of the fact that Shraddha is not in the hall. With time he starts to notice just how happy he is with her and how clear his mind is right now, he is not thinking about anything right now, his body is moving on its own, all he can see is Shweta, and all he can think is Shweta. Shweta is happy, she didn't know playing can be fun and fulfilling or is it the company she is enjoying? She is developing more and more feelings for him but being the stubborn girl, she is still not ready to accept that. She puts aside the complicated stuff and enjoys the fun she's having while playing the game and perhaps "the game with him". Every now and then Shivansh loses a point or two just to see her smile, and even laugh if he gets lucky. Those little gestures she shows when she scores after long rallies are a cure to his heart.

Finally, Shweta gets tired again but doesn't want to ask for a break again. Shivansh being the gentleman, says, 'Aren't you tired? Let's take a break.'

'Sure, if you are that tired…' she says trying her best to not show that she's out of breath.

'Yes, ma'am I am tired, I cannot play anymore. I want some water.' He says with a smirk.

They both put down their rackets on the table and for the first time notice that there is no one else in the hall.

'Where's Shraddha?' they ask in sync, after a long pause with no answer to their common question they start laughing. Shivansh has always loved to see her laugh, her voice makes the perfect scores of melodies, and her prepossessing eyes get covered by her delicate eyelids.

I wonder, why her face is made in this shape? Why is it that I feel happy when I watch her? How is it that a face that makes me so happy is in front of me?

Shivansh doesn't say anything, maybe he can't. She goes and sits on the bench. Takes out her water bottle and asks him to sit, offering the bottle, like she always does. After catching their breath, they go outside to find Shraddha. She is right outside looking at the mountains.

'When did you leave? You could've at least told us?' says Shweta.

'I did but you two were so immersed in each other that you didn't hear me.'

This makes Shweta blush, and after a long pause, she replies, 'What are you talking about? We were just playing. Maybe we couldn't hear you because of the sound of the ball…'

Shivansh really enjoys watching her like this. Her cheeks and ears take half a second to turn red.

They have played for about two hours and are sitting idle for quite a while, making fun of each other and laughing. Shweta lives quite far so they start to head back. Sun starts to get closer to the horizon and cast a vermilion hue on the clouds. Their faces are lit up in the same warm light, and they hurry to reach the place for Shweta to catch the bus. Shraddha just cannot give up doing something nice for them, she starts to act like she's tired and cannot go any faster.

'You can sit here for a while if you are tired, I'll go with her' says Shivansh.

'Please do that otherwise she might miss the bus,' she says still breathing a little heavy, of course fake.

She's such a great friend! Thinks Shweta and Shivansh at the same time.

They leave, leaving Shraddha behind, with no guilt at all. How would they feel anything else with everything going on in their minds? *Should I hold her hand or is it too soon?* Shivansh looks at her as if he's asking to hold her hand with his eyes only. Shweta's too shy to look at him right now.

'Shweta?'

'Yes?' she looks at him and smiles.

'You are getting late don't you think?' he says and grabs her hand and starts running. *What the hell! I really did it and I wasn't even ready. The way she looked at me just now, the way she smiled, I had no clue what to say next. It all happened in an instant, but I don't hate it. At all.*

OMG! OMG! OMG! Where did that come from? Relax Shweta, he is just trying to get you there on time, Isn't he?

Both, not knowing what to say, remain quiet, running and panting. Just when they see the bus, Shweta stops running, 'I can't look we're already here. Let's walk now.'

'Yeah... sure...' says Shivansh, panting lightly.

After catching their breath, they continue to walk towards the bus. Getting on the bus seemed like a very tough job to do, tougher than homework. They both wait for the bus to start to delay the time to leave each other.

'So, you coming tomorrow or are you giving up?' says Shivansh, trying to cheer up the mood.

'Of course, I'll come, why wouldn't I? You think I am going to give up?'

'No, that's not what I meant, just kidding. Good to know you'll be here.'

'I'll come to pick you up...' the engine noise interrupts him, he goes louder, 'I'll be waiting for you right here, same time.'

Shweta takes a step on the bus only to realise they haven't left each other's hand. Shivansh wants to pull her, but he knows he can't, he lets go of her hand and shows a smile and a lingering wave. She waves back with a forced smile.

At home, Shivansh thinks about how complete his day went. *I just cannot wait to see her tomorrow. It'll be more fun when she gets a little better. Maybe I'll let her win a set or two, but not easily she'll have to work for it, and then I'll get to see her brightest smile.* Sleep embraces him slowly but firmly, being tired after a long day surely makes one dream more vivid.

The last day was pure bliss for him and seeing Shweta again at the same time after school makes today great as well. Cherry on top, Shraddha isn't here, not that her presence is *annoying or anything* but her not being here means more time he has with Shweta and Shweta alone.

Time continues to pass by unnoticed, Shivansh continues to wait for Shweta, they both take a walk to the hall, meeting up with Shraddha, playing and learning the game, getting to know more about one another with each passing day, and becoming a certified trio.

The day has arrived to show what they have learnt since the day they started going to play, Shweta has never participated in any sports activity, and naturally, she's nervous. Shivansh tries to throw a couple of jokes, not working. Shraddha says, 'What a cute couple, he's trying so hard just to cheer you up.'

'What couple? You just say whatever you want Shraddha. I'm not talking to you anymore,' says Shweta loudly, trying to hide her shyness.

'When nothing works, there comes a saviour named Shraddha' says Shivansh, noticing how her nervousness diluted.

'And why were you even nervous? My match is first, look at me, do I look like I'm nervous?'

'No, but soon my match will be there, won't it be? And I can't play that well, I might lose…' says Shweta in a low tone.

'So?'

'Who likes to lose?'

'Do you know just how many times you lost to me?'

'No…'

'Did you feel sad? Or was it not fun?'

'It was, it was fun but that's different, isn't it? I played with you two.'

'And we both are here, so buckle up, you are not going to lose and even if you do lose, you'll have fun losing. I think they are calling my name;

I should go. All the best.' Shivansh runs off in the direction his name is being called.

The first match is over. Shivansh wins. He comes out to tell them, but it seems like the news arrived before him.

'See! I told you I'd win,' he says with a smug face.

'We know you are good but don't get too full of yourself, it would have been pretty comic to see your face if you had lost,' says Shweta and they all start to laugh.

'Sadly, you won't get to see that face because I am going to win. I don't have much competition you see,' he says still laughing.

'It's good that you are confident, at least you are not scared as hell like someone else here,' says Shraddha pushing her elbow into Shweta.

'I'm not scared!' says Shweta in a not-so-convincing voice.

'It's fine to be afraid Shweta, nothing to be embarrassed about. Also, you've been practising with us for the past two weeks. You are among the best players here.' says Shivansh to make her feel better and before he can say more, Shraddha gets called for her match. It's her first match.

Shraddha vs Shivani. Shraddha wins.

Since the small school can only manage one table for playing, both boys' and girls' matches are being played on the same table alternatively. As soon as Shraddha comes out of the hall, next boys' match is started. All three are winning match after match only to find each other in finals. Everyone is allowed to have a short break before the two final matches are played. The rest of the school excluding the primary classes is summoned to watch and cheer in the finals.

'Shraddha, go and fetch the trophy for our house,' says Shivansh walking towards his fellow finalists.

'So, you are on her side. Okay...' says Shweta.

'Of course, I mean, we are in the same team basically' he teases back.

'What did you think Shweta? What do you want him to do?' Shraddha joins him.

'He should have...' Shweta rolls her eyes and after a short pause says, '...just stayed quiet.'

Shivansh and Shraddha laugh their hearts out, Shweta doesn't find this funny, at all. He loves to see that look on her face, a little jealous, a little annoyed, and immeasurably cute. *Who thought I'd be able to see these expressions when she's such a cute kid?* I cannot help but keep teasing her, sometimes it just happens on its own. He goes again and keeps saying some things that are surely going to make Shweta more annoyed.

Both of them try their best to get her back in a good mood but nothing seems to work. *I knew it was going to be nearly impossible to cheer her up after teasing her for so long! Whatever we say now it's all useless, but at least I got to see that cute face of hers, it was all worth it. And since she's not so much into winning this thing I think, I hope, she's going to calm down in a while. Ah! I don't even want to play the next match; I just want to keep looking at her. What do I do? It's not like that match is that important, maybe I can just skip it and let the guy in the final win by default. Yeah, that sounds like a nice idea, I can do that. So, I'm not going anywhere. I am staying here only.*

'Where are Shweta and Shraddha? It's time for the girl's final' shouts the Manoj from afar.

Both of them leave Shivansh lost in thought and start running towards the hall. He snaps out and runs behind them. *Maybe that wasn't that good of an idea...* Shweta doesn't look annoyed anymore, she looks focused. Beaming with confidence, Shraddha doesn't even need someone to say something to her, she's ready for the match.

They both take their positions, and the match starts. Shivansh, despite what he said, roots for Shweta to win. He cannot let others see that though; what a bind he is in, cheering for Shraddha and rooting for Shweta. She played well, actually far better than he ever imagined but like he knew the outcome, Shraddha won the final match. She jumps in happiness, while Shweta not being a sore loser, is neither frustrated nor sad. She's just happy that her friend won and the game being out of her area of expertise helped too. All that remains now is the boys' final.

Just like the girls' final match, everybody is watching the boys' final match too. A lot of cheering for Shivansh is coming loud from the crowd, his friends, his teammates, and even some teachers. *Man, I missed being everyone's favourite. If not favourite, then somewhat popular. Childhood wasn't so bad... Especially here. Is she watching? Where is she?*

He looks around to find that one pair of eyes looking at him. He sees her, looking at him with clasped hands. She somewhat knows that he's going to win but cannot help but be worried. She whispers, 'You better win!' in the loveliest way possible. It's not like he was nervous or doubtful if he'd win but seeing her lips move in that specific way, he feels a surge of confidence that he'll not only win this match but the world if she ever asks him to.

He brings back his attention to the match, he knows the opponent, and he knows that he's going to win. *Should I make this a little more interesting? What happens if I lose the first set and then win the rest two? I have always wanted to do this! I think this might be the perfect opportunity to show off in front of so many people and in such an overpowered way. But! Ah! I hate this! I can't do that; most people here already know that I play well, and I think it'll be a little too much. Well, that settles it then. I'm gonna play without holding back. Sorry bro, you lost last time, and you are going to lose even worse this time.*

The match starts and points start to roll towards Shivansh's side one after another. Set two ends with the victory in his favour. It was easy for everyone to guess the winner of the final, yet it seemed like they enjoyed the game despite knowing the outcome. Shraddha jumps in excitement, Shweta wants to run and hug Shivansh but can't, Shivansh isn't as excited as others, he is just happy, he is more interested in knowing what the one he cares about thinks about all of it. All three head outside to leave behind the crowd and the noise.

'Congratulations, Shivansh. You did win after all' says Shraddha.

'Did you think I was being overconfident and saying stuff like that? I meant it.' Responds annoyed Shivansh.

'I kinda knew he would,' says Shweta.

'Oh, really?' says Shraddha with a smirk.

'I mean we both knew he plays well, to the point that it wouldn't be surprising if he wins the tournament.'

'Well, to be honest, I didn't think it was impossible for him to win but I had my doubts. He kept saying that that was the first time he even held the TT racket yet, he was so confident, unbelievable!'

'Exactly! That's what I was thinking but seeing him play did make me believe that he could win nevertheless.'

He quietly watches them talk endlessly. He can see that Shweta is excited to grab the second position, she was never into sports yet getting a medal was more than she could ask for. As instructed, everyone begins to head back to their classes. Hall slowly becomes increasingly empty, the surroundings becoming quieter.

Shraddha again makes a favourable move for Shivansh and leaves them for *something* she has to do. They start to walk, Shivansh is looking at her, listening to her. She tells him everything about how her matches went, how scared she sometimes was, and how she felt about winning sets and even matches. In the final match, she was pretty sure that Shraddha would win, but she gave it her all, and she has no regrets.

'So, we are not going to practice in the evening anymore? She says with a gloomy voice, her eyes looking at her feet.

'Yeah…' he doesn't know what to say, all he knows is that he cannot ask her to come so far from her home just to play with him, every day, and for no other reason. In his heart, he knows that it was nice that they got to spend so much time together for days, but this cannot go on forever and one day which happens to be today, it ends. From tomorrow, everything will go back to usual. He can only see Shweta in the school, they can only get a little improvised time here and there to talk to each other without anyone around.

I'm sure Shraddha will help me out but there's only so much she can do. No matter what I do, it is going to be hard to get some time with her and that too will not even be close to the time we had until now. It was surely great and quite unexpected, to be honest. Gotta be happy with what I got and think about what to do next! All right, so much already happened, I think I can manage in the future too.

They reach the door, and Shweta is still talking and the way she is going, she is not going to stop soon. He leans his back against the wall outside the class and she keeps going on and on. He loves to see her talk, the way her face perfectly shows what she's feeling, the way her tiny hands move in a certain way, the way her eyes twinkle when she talks about something that makes her happy. *I wish there comes a day when her eyes look like this when she talks about me.*

'Teachers are coming down the stairs, on your seats if you don't want to get scolded right after you won' says Shraddha after finally coming when she noticed the teachers heading back to continue their classes.

Shivansh and Shweta rush to their respective seat in an instant. Shraddha does the same after them. Seated, they look at each other's faces and laugh, unnoticed in the noise of chatter. Without much delay, the teacher arrives and starts the class without wasting much time.

While leaving school, they start to walk together, silently. From today, Shweta won't be coming for the practice. To lift up the mood Shivansh says, 'You'll receive the medal tomorrow, you know that right?'

'Yes…' say both Shweta and Shraddha with a long sigh.

'Aren't you excited? Shraddha you were so gung-ho about this, you even dragged me into this, not that I didn't like it, but you did. And Shweta, you got yourself second place even though you weren't even that interested. So, cheer up you two. You look horrible like this.' He laughs wanting them to join him as well and they do. The awkward mood slightly shifts as they continue to laugh.

Evening, Shivansh goes to play with his friends like he used to except for the last two weeks. Today, he is playing basketball, with all of his friends, yet feels a little lonely. It is about time when Shweta would come and join him and Shraddha to play table tennis but not today, not today onwards. Unlike earlier, it doesn't feel like the time has passed in the blink of an eye, it seems to have grown, and the sun is taking too long to come down. Unlike any other day he wants to go home early but to him, it feels like the match has been going on for hours yet, it never ends, he is tired, tired of it all.

'I need to go home early today,' he says and passes the ball to Aakash, and leaves the court.

'Right now? We haven't even played for an hour. Why are you going so early?'

'I told you I needed to go back early today. I have some work to do.' He says in a low tone.

Aakash notices something is off with him. 'I'll be back in a while; you all keep playing.' He says to everyone and leaves the ball in the middle of the court, and goes to Shivansh.

'Can you do me this favour and tell me what happened? Why don't you want to play today? Something happened?'

'Nah, I just don't feel like playing today.'

'So, it was not about *some work at home.* It was about Shweta all along.'

'What? NO!'

'C'mon, don't you think it's useless to hide it from me?'

'Hiding what,' says Shivansh and tries to laugh it off.

'So, you can talk about Shraddha but I can't talk about Shweta? Believe me, you two are way more obvious' Aakash persists. Now, it has come down to friendship, Shivansh can no longer hide it from him.

'Yes, it is… you are right. Happy?'

'I knew it. You like her, don't you?'

'More than that' he says with no sign of hesitation in his voice, his eyes beaming with clarity.

'Okay, this is pretty serious. I didn't know. And yes, I'm going to tell everyone about this.' He laughs.

Shivansh punches him in the gut, a typical boys thing, 'Don't you dare!'

They both start to laugh hard, together.

'So, you really are not going to play, are you?' Aakash asks, hoping that he stays.

'Yeah, not today. Not in the mood. Maybe tomorrow.'

Shivansh leaves.

'You are early. Don't tell me you again got injured while playing. I always tell you to take it easy, but you never listen' says Pooja as Shivansh enters the house.

'Maa, I'm not injured. I just didn't want to play more. So, I came back.' He replies as he takes a seat and starts to untie his shoelaces. The last thing he wants to do is to study today, he goes into the living room, turns on the television and waits for dinner so he can get into his bed as soon as possible.

Turning sides, he again struggles to sleep.

New day which means another day to go to school and meet her, he wakes up with a smile and rushes with all the chores to reach school at the earliest. He finds himself standing in front of school gates, closed. *I guess I should have waited a little longer to leave. I hope something like the keys getting misplaced happens and the gate remains closed for a while when she comes. We can then have a little chat before we start the school. Once we get into class, it is only going to get harder to get that luxury. And yeah, we are going to get awarded today. I hope I get a photo with her. Lucky day!*

His thoughts become reality as he finds her getting off the bus. Both faces light up the moment their eyes meet. She waves her tiny hand to say hello and reaches the gate. He leans back on the gate as they start to talk.

As usual, Shivansh does not have much to say but to look at her. Seeing her move her tiny hands in cute ways, getting tired of the heavy bag she has and adjusting it again and again, her eyes shine bewitchingly in the direct early morning sunlight, her complexion looking ever so slightly golden from the sunlight and bright red from the cold, *is there even a word for a colour like this,* he thinks. As expected, certainly not wanted, other students come, and the gate is also open to let everyone inside. They have to go to their class and sit and study, just not talk like they want to. But before all that, they have to attend the assembly, and after assembly, prizes for the TT tournament will be given. Something Shivansh is looking forward to.

After prayer, Manoj calls winners to assemble beside the stage. One by one, Mrs Pushpa hands a medal and a certificate with a lovely smile, and a photo is taken as well.

'Third prize goes to Neha,' Manoj announces.

'Second prize goes to Shweta.'

Shweta, struggling to suppress her happiness, goes onto the stage with a wide smile and cherry-like cheeks, and receives the medal.

'And the first prize goes to Shraddha,' she goes with confidence, she is happy, but her aura is different from Shweta's. Shweta was so happy to get the second place, like it happened by luck but Shraddha radiates the aura that tells everyone looking at her that she has earned it by her hard work and talent.

'Moving on to boys' tournament, third prize goes to Rahul.'

'Second prize goes to Ravi.'

'And the first prize goes to Shivansh,' he walks onto the stage looking at Shweta to see her reaction. She is still smiling the way she was smiling when she received her medal, clapping non-stop. Embarrassingly enough, he keeps looking at her and even Pushpa says, 'Where are you looking, Shivansh? Look at the camera, don't you want a photo?'

'Yes, Ma'am I do. Sorry, I was a little distracted.' He turns his face to the camera and smiles.

Then comes the time he's been waiting for days, a photo with Shweta. It is going to be a group photo but it's something. Since he and Shraddha received the first prize, they took a position right beside Pushpa. Shraddha wants to switch places with Shweta but struggles to decide if she should do it or not, then just one look at Shivansh's face makes her choose what she wants to do and not care about anything else. Everyone who received a medal gathers around, Pushpa is in the centre, Shivansh on her right side and Shweta on her left, close to each other, in their first photo together. The photographer says, 'Cheese!' and takes around 10 pictures to have a perfect click. In seven of them, Shivansh is not looking at the camera, at all.

Coming back to their class, they find themselves walking with no one but each other, thanks to Shraddha who made up an excuse to go to the bathroom at the right time. Shivansh wants to thank her for showing these caring gestures whenever possible. Shweta is enjoying a lot talking about her matches and how unbelievably good she played despite being her first time participating in something like this.

'You didn't mind what I said earlier, did you?' says Shivansh, something he was holding inside for a long time.

'What exactly are you talking about right now...?' she says as she doesn't even know what he is talking about.

'So, you are mad at me!'

'No, not really. I mean I understand that you both are in the same team and of course, you'd support her so, what's there to be mad about? And why would I get mad at you of all people.'

Ugh! That "at you of all people" hurts a lot, doesn't it? 'All right, at least you agree now that you are in fact mad at me. So, madam, tell me what can I do to make you accept my apology?'

'I'm not mad I told you!' she raises her voice enough to make her point and not bring anyone else's attention but at the same time tries to hide her smile. *Madam! Did he just call me madam? Oh god! He is so stupid!*

'Okay, I won't press further but you are mad at me, a little bit I think.'

'Whatever…'

'You won't be for long. You can't.'

'Really? We'll see about that.'

'I'm kidding you know that, right? Right? And I am definitely not challenging you, okay?'

She grins at him as they enter the class and take their seats. A teacher can come anytime now but no one is quiet. Chanchal dashes in and starts rubbing the blackboard, pin-drop-silence spreads in an instant, the way most teachers can only dream of.

It's Monday morning yet, Shivansh finds himself in high spirits. All because he spent his Sunday doing one thing he wanted to do, being with the one person he wanted to be with, Shweta.

Some girls are playing some game, surrounding the teacher's table. Others are busy talking; it is chilly outside so almost no one is outside. Winds play with sound as they pass through the pine trees, it feels like someone is trying really hard to whistle but all the effort is in vain. Shivansh enjoys talking to his friends, leaning on the side of a bench while others are sitting, and some are standing. It is lunchtime, and everybody is doing their own thing, he knows Shweta went outside but he can't just follow her around all the time, others can get suspicious. And he is enjoying the time he is having with his old friends, just talking and laughing and roasting each other feels so good he can't believe how much he used to enjoy this time of his life.

Lost in thought, he stares at the ceiling when Aakash brings him back to reality, 'It has become his usual for quite some time.' He looks at him and finds out that Shraddha is standing in front of him. *When did she come? Wait! Is this what I think it is? No way! I can't believe this is happening exactly the way it happened last time even though so much has changed. What should I do now, I know what she is going to do...*

'Sorry!' she says and bam! Shraddha is a girl who can land a solid smack. Before he could decide what to do it was done. Last time, he would have slapped any girl back without a second thought but not her so, he didn't. He did something even worse that had begun to plague their friendship. He had to let it out somehow so, he went to their class teacher and told her about the "game" the girls were playing and how he ended up getting slapped for no reason at all or just for fun. Shraddha hated that, maybe even more than she would have hated a slap back from him. No way the adult Shivansh can even think of going to a teacher after this like a child. So, what can he even do? What should he do? After two lengthiest seconds he says, 'I can't just say it's alright, no problem, can I?' with a smile.

Shraddha doesn't know what to say, she waits for him to continue.

'An eye for an eye, a slap for a slap and especially for a slap this hard.' He straightens up and gets close to her, lifting his hand. She knows it's coming. She can't move, she is going to get slapped, probably a lot harder than he did. She instinctively closes her eyes the moment his hand is about to swing. Almost everyone in the class is looking at them, thanks to the sound her slap made. To her and everyone else's surprise, he doesn't hit her back but gives her a gentle tap on her cheek and says, 'We are even now.' *Damn! Why is everyone so surprised? Did they really think I was going to hit her?*

She has no clue what to do now, she just smiles back at him awkwardly and goes back to her group, turning around to look at him again and again. Shivansh is euphoric, not only he handled the situation way better than he could have imagined but all the other things were, so far, going the way, he wanted. Yes, he did get a tight slap right across his face but in some way, it was worth it, what happened after that must have poured some points to him from everybody in the class and his friendship with Shraddha won't be ruined like it did back in the day.

He hangs the group photo of the winners in his room, him gawking at Shweta in the photo, and hopes to add more and more photos to the wall as time goes by.

CHAPTER 08: HER BIRTHDAY

It's already December! Thinks Shivansh with a broad smile on his face, he can barely keep himself from jumping. *Her birthday is only a few days away, what should I do? So far, I've been doing good enough, no, more than good enough. I've been scoring well, playing well and I think I have gained a few kilos. The days I spent with her were better than I had hoped for. Thank goodness she didn't start skipping school like she used to do in college.* Shweta looks buried under layers and layers of clothes every time she is spotted.

It is freezing but beautiful, fewer people come outside, and the sky is saturated with clouds, leaving little to no room for sunshine to descend and deliver warmth. Evenings are more vivid; pinks are rosier, and the sun is even redder. Mornings are bliss, as pretty as one can fathom, more often than not, snowflakes fall in slow motion and beautify every bit of earth they touch.

But with December comes winter and with winter comes the winter vacation, and that means he has to live two months without getting a chance to look at her let alone be with her. And he has no way of contacting her since he can't muster up the courage to ask her number. *What excuse can I even make to justify asking for her number? Homework? That is so not going to work in a million years.* With this going over in his head all the time, their conversations start to die sooner, Shweta knows that something has been bugging him for some time, making him behave in an unusual way, more unusual than his regular unusual. Even she feels some uneasiness in her heart but she can't tell if it's his behaviour that is making her feel that way or the thought that they won't be talking to each other for as long as two months. They both can't bring themselves to talk about the matter and as the day comes closer, tension between them increases.

To provide himself with something to think about and look forward to after the holidays he comes up with a plan. It is the last day of school, and he accompanies her to the bus. Both walk as voiceless as they can be. She starts to climb up the stairs, still thinking about something to say but it is useless. She takes her usual seat and looks at him. He smiles, the moment she sees, she knows that either he is about to do something, or he might have already done something. He can't hold back any longer and shouts, 'Check your bag!'.

'No, you DID not just,' she pulls the zipper on her bag and starts to explore her bag, knowing that there is something in her bag that she is unaware of. Her hand touches something wrapped in cute plastic paper with some cartoons drawn over it and her eyes spot a piece of paper stuck on it. Instantaneously, her lips lose their capability to hide her teeth, and her cheeks cannot hold the blood rushing into them to make her face as red as a rose. She smiles, to see such an honest expression on her face he knows that all the hard work he did was worth it.

She struggles to choose what to do now, she looks at him. His radiant smile waits for her, for her to say something, for her to do something but what should she do, what could she do now? *God! I have no idea! He's definitely waiting for me to say something.* He is not. He knows how she reacts in situations like these, he is just enjoying the way she's so happy and tense at the same time, just to say something. He raises his hands above his waist level and acts as if he is reading a book. Not knowing what else to do, she looks back at the unexpected present in her bag and the note on it, and starts reading.

Hey Shweta,

I know it's way ahead of time but Happy Birthday! I'll be leaving for my hometown tomorrow, so I won't be able to wish you the very day. I wanted to say sorry for the uneasiness and weird moments every now and then for the past few days, but I guess this just shows how close we have become and honestly, I want to be even closer to you.

I have a really hard-to-do request for you but I know you can do it; can you open it on the day of your birthday? Please? I know you know that there's a book inside, couldn't find a box in time, but at least you don't know which book, I hope. I'll be glad if you can hold yourself for a few days. I don't have anything else to say, you can do whatever feels right. See you after the holidays.

-Shivansh

'I'll try' she says with a grin.

'Please do try!' he shouts at the top of his lungs to overpower the noise of the engine.

The bus moves taking away Shweta from him for a long time. Swinging her hand, she yells, 'Have a safe journey back home, see ya!'

He waves back and turns back to crawl his way back home, head hanging down, staring at his shoes. He again lives through the mixed feelings he felt for the first time when they had to go back home, hundreds of kilometres away. He's happy to have done something to make her smile and *make her happy* but the void she leaves when she goes away seems larger today. *Is it because I'm not going to see her for days or is it because I won't be here for her birthday? I did everything I could so, why do I feel this way? Nothing is in my hands...*

On a train of thoughts, he goes places and memories. The ceiling seems to slowly fall over him, he is floating. Images pour harder into his mind, the ceiling, the walls, the bed, and the table start to morph. He is in his hostel now, where he studied in his high school. He was in 12th standard when he realised and accepted that he was not really the emotional type, he did laugh aloud and yell in anger but he could no longer feel the peak of any emotion, it felt fake, no matter how happy or sorrowful he felt it only lasted for a moment, after that he would become as calm as dead, as if there was nothing get happy or sad about in the first place. Empathy seemed like a dream to him, *how can one truly understand someone else's pain, joy, rage, or anything? How do I even react to these things, especially when someone gets vulnerable in front of me just to get heard?* The realisation did hit him pretty hard but he realised that the same thing made him come out of that shock in a moment and he was calm again, just like always.

To him everyone else around him was a hot-blooded idiot, getting angry or happy over every little thing while he remained mostly in the same mood but then he knew that it was he who was the cold-blooded one, a living robot, to react to anything. And he came to terms with it, with himself, there was nothing he could do about it and nothing be solved by worrying.

But then came you... a thought comes in his mind, that draws him out of his misery just like she did a decade ago. He feels better, not worried about tomorrow. *I have waited for years, what's a silly vacation to me? And as I promised, I'm going to enjoy this time of my life.* But he still cannot sleep, he dives back again into the memories of how he got in contact with her again after 8 years after leaving Nainital. He was in his final year, doing civil engineering, far from her in Kota, the city of dreams.

Their story didn't go like most other couples, they didn't start talking day and night only to end up in love and a relationship. Having a lot to share about, the first conversation was indeed long. Telling each other about how they spent their last 8 years and how they finally found themselves where they were at that time.

After that, they hardly ever talked daily, sending each other some memes, and suggesting web shows, which could add a couple more minutes to their talks. She mentioned Korean and Chinese web shows more than anything and how pretty their characters were, on the other hand, he was into anime.

On one average evening, which was not at all average for Shivansh, Shweta texts him saying she had watched the anime he recommended to her, Hori-Miya. And how she loved it.

> Everyone wants a boyfriend like Miyamura but nobody gets one.

> Try me

> Are you serious?
>
> Would you choose me?
>
> You hardly know me

"Try me" two words he typed for a laugh, two words that she took seriously and the two words that would change everything. He knew that she was taking this seriously, but he wanted to go further, it was thrilling and funny, sort of. He knew that the conversation from this point on would be pretty interesting and at the end, he would just tell her how he meant it as a joke but continued to talk like that for fun. But things didn't go as planned, the more they talked, the more she argued about how she might not be the right person for him, and the more he told her how she was the only one and he liked everything about her, giving her a counter to everything she said against them dating he began to realise, he actually liked her. It was miraculous that he never thought about it but now that she was making him say all this stuff to "prove" his love, he discovered that everything he was spouting was not nonsense but true, deep in his heart, someplace that he was unaware of its existence. That's how he ended up telling her how he felt about her in a not so "confession of love" way.

That was the first turning point in their lives. She did want to say "no" to him but being a good person, she couldn't bring herself to break his heart with an outright rejection. Instead, she asked him to wait, wait for her to know more about him and sort her feelings, hoping that he would eventually get tired of waiting and give up.

From that day, they went from "sharing memes sometimes" to "talking daily for hours". Shivansh, like any other young boy fell in love for the first time, and was ready to wait for years for his love, not exactly how she planned but she did like talking to him. It was not hard to talk to him, she could tell him anything, she never felt bored, and she started to look up to having another chat with him.

Maybe she loved him too… He understood that she had a lot on her plate right now. She needed to focus on her college exams and career. The last thing she would want is to lose everything just figuring out if she wanted to be in a relationship. And he would wait for all of this to get over, where she would have nothing to worry about when she could think freely, feel what's inside her heart and tell him her final answer. Having his feelings confessed, he could then talk more freely, he had no trump cards left. He didn't need to try various things to impress her or give her hints to let her know how he felt without actually telling her.

Conversations got more frequent and lengthier. Shivansh being a sucker at chatting, took the help of the internet more often than not to keep the convo captivating. "How to keep talking without getting awkward", "Top 10 questions to ask your crush", "Top 10 questions to ask before dating", "How to know if she likes you", "How to sound romantic without sounding like a creep" and what not, then to hand pick the best questions among the top 10 questions to ask her. With time, he stopped looking for *topics* and *questions,* it became easier just to not hang up and spend hours talking to each other, sometimes even when they wanted to stop, they couldn't. There was nothing they couldn't talk about, from deep conversations to silly talks, from teasing her to telling her what she meant for him, from getting angry over childish stuff to sharing their dreams, from telling their biggest strengths to their deepest insecurities.

This new phase in their life was certainly magical, they started to find coincidences that seemed more like fate, how one's strength compensates for another's weakness, and how their day became more about thinking of another than anything else.

But everything has to end at some point and so ended Shivansh's patience for his love, his days went from shiny, flowery and warm to hopeless waiting and suffering, alone and cold. To him, she was giving mixed hints, sometimes it felt like she did like him back and sometimes it felt like she didn't. Uncertainty can make people go mad in matters of love and he was getting drained of all his oxygen from his lungs, and heartache was not bearable anymore. So, he decided to ask her out for one last time. After this, if she said yes then he would be the happiest man on earth and if she said no then no matter what would happen to his heart, he would stop trying to get her and move on with his life, focus on his studies, career, basically, get back to his old life.

28th August 2021, was the date he decided to confess his feelings one last time and get a definitive answer. Luck, being his archnemesis, played a little game to mess up his plan once again. It all happened so suddenly and at such an unexpected time, he was not ready for this, he was not ready to tell her that he likes her. It was night, they were chatting after dinner. She was telling him all about her day, the way he liked to listen to every day. Shweta couldn't talk about anything close to love and relationships since he had confessed to her. And he didn't want to talk about that either till the day came when he asked her for real. As always though, they were comfortable and having a good time talking to each other.

He told her that he would go and brush his teeth before bed, or else he would not be able to get up once he gets too cozy in his bed.

Nevertheless, she kept texting him, making him struggle between the two. She told him about a meme she saw a few days back and that she liked it so much that she had saved it on her phone. Before he could text back anything as simple as "Hmm" she sent the meme.

His brush stopped moving, his eyes widened, and all his sleep flew away in an instant. He had no idea how to respond.

You know what, I saw this meme. I loved it

Wait, let me send it to you

Life is short, Propose me

He couldn't tell if his brain was overclocking or completely shut. Being an overthinker he couldn't stop the rush of thousands of thoughts and scenarios in his head.

What was she even thinking while or before sending this meme? Is she serious right now? Is she joking? Is she making fun of me? Did she just send an average fun meme that I am thinking too much about? Most of all, what does she expect me to reply to this now? What do I say? What can I say? Should I just laugh it off with some laughing emojis? No! what if she is serious? Should I scrap that plan and ask her out right now? Ughhh! But what if it's just a meme, nothing more? Amidst all these unending deliberations, he finally decided on something worth texting her back. He believed that could be perfect to handle both the situations of her being serious and joking. 4 minutes had passed, and he texted back.

This was the best reply he could think of in all his capability, but he would soon find out that he was way off beam. And then the texts were sent from both sides, but it was far from the best talks they had had earlier.

> When?

> > When I told you everything about how I felt, you are asking "When?"!

> But you didn't ask me to date you!

> > Is that any different? (genuinely confused)

> Just leave it! You ruined it!

> > I don't know what to say. I couldn't even believe you were being serious. Heck, I can't even now. We were just joking around and then I told you that I was brushing and then you suddenly

sent that meme. I just thought you were either joking or maybe even teasing me.

I cannot pull such a big joke. I don't have that capacity

Alright. I'm sorry. I misunderstood and yeah, I sort of ruined it but I promise I'll make it up to you by doing this the right way

I don't think so Mr Shivansh

Believe me, I'll do something about it. Just try and forget about this. And don't expect anything anytime soon. Okay?

Whatever

> I will surely make it up to you, you just keep everything "normal", okay?

> Please don't do something grand, I hate that.

> Don't you tell me what to do! And you know that I know.

His eyes feel dry and burning. It is five in the morning. *I can't believe I didn't sleep all night!* He turns to his left side, facing the wall, and closes his eyes, they hurt but he keeps them closed.

Pooja moves the curtains to let the sunlight fill the room. That burns his eyes, having slept for only 3 hours, he pleads, 'Maa, please! It's a holiday. Lemme sleep'

'No! Look outside it's practically noon. Wake up beta…'

He looks at the clock with his eyes still almost closed, still burning, and says, 'Maa, it's only 8! Let me sleep for another hour or two. Please!'

'But the breakfast is waiting for you, beta. Just wake up for now, have your breakfast and then I'll let you sleep for as much as you want. Okay?'

He struggles to get out of his bed and navigate himself to the washroom, washes his face with chilled water. He's finally able to open his eyes without the burning sensation.

As soon as he finishes up with his breakfast, he starts doing his homework. *Who wants to waste their entire vacations doing homework? I already have things to worry about. I hope she likes the book…* They are leaving today, and he does not want to carry his books and notebooks on the way. Being the exemplary Indian parents, they are both pretty happy to see their elder son with his books. However, Tarun also gets trapped in this.

'Look at your brother, learn something from him. All day TV and games. If you want to watch your cartoons, then you better stick to your desk for 2 hours straight' says Pooja.

Annoyed Tarun leaves the room without saying anything, knowing it will only work against him. Shivansh is proceeding quite fast with his homework, he got quite the head start before the vacation even started, while the naughty little Tarun stares at his book, pretending to study. An hour has passed, Vivek gets bored watching the debate on television about some random agenda and goes to the other to check on the two. Without entering, he peeps from behind the curtain only to witness both of them studying. He returns to the living room, smiling.

Lunch is on the lighter side today since they are leaving in 4 hours, a 30-hour journey with the headache of changing buses and trains to finally reach the remote location of their hometown. Tarun gets to watch TV like Pooja promised. Shivansh is closer to completing his homework.

They leave at 5:18 pm, 18 minutes late! Everyone is aware not to say or do something stupid to get Vivek mad, the family takes their first bus and Vivek puts the larger trolley bag in the trunk of the bus. Feeling a bit nostalgic, he enjoys his ride to the fullest except for the part where he pukes twice on the moving bus. Lunch is gone and he is quite hungry again but cannot dare to eat anything. At least he gets to have the window seat, and he starts to look at the mountains, the rivers, the trees, and the animals. Nothing about this feels less than amazing.

The bus moves along the perfect course at the perfect time when the sunset can be seen, the view is phenomenal, and the distant mountains are covered in snow looking like the closest thing to heaven, one of the passengers, maybe a tourist, takes photos with her DSLR and shows it to her friend. *I think she got quite the picture;* he thinks looking at their faces in awe. It starts to get a little dark and the temperature falls rapidly, people start to close their windows and some even start to wear their woollen caps.

It's time to get off the bus, Pooja wakes Shivansh and Tarun and takes them outside the bus, and Vivek gets the luggage. They need to get to the station and wait for the train; while waiting, they decide to have dinner. Both the siblings are feeling sleepy, Pooja makes them wash their faces and sit. Getting on the train is a challenge on its own, getting the kids inside, getting the luggage, and all of it while dealing with the crowd. Once they get on their reserved seats, Shivansh and Tarun go to sleep.

They arrive at the destination the next day at 10:00 pm. Both the brothers drink only a glass of milk before they go to bed, exhausted from the extended journey.

Pooja doesn't wake the boys for another two hours after waking up. Shivansh gets up and goes outside stretching his arms high in the air. Measly sunlight reaches the fields through the thick fog, the farm is divided into three sections, white fog, yellow flowers of mustard and green stems. He has always missed this, this cold, this crop, this inability to see far, this sensation on his nose and cheek, this joy he used to get when he was able to see his warm breath and pretend, he was smoking, and this mud stove he used to sit nearby in the morning and before going to bed. Technically, it is after 7 years, he is here at this time of the year, from the time when he was a working adult.

Right after having a glass of milk the boys ask their grandpa if they can go out and play cricket, and there is no one in the house to overpower his authority so, Vivek and Pooja just watch them leave. He is having the time of his life playing cricket in his hometown after so long, it is the same sport but feels a whole lot different from the way he is used to play in Nainital.

Having not much to do after the game and having a lengthy gossip with his grandparents, he gets back to his holiday homework. After all the hard work, he couldn't complete his homework and had to bring English and Hindi notebooks, *how can one write 40 pages of "Good Handwriting" in both languages in such a short time?* He thinks cursing his teachers. Writing everything he sees in the book next to him; he counts the days to her birthday. 12 days, and in 12 days she will turn 13 on December 18.

If it all goes with his plan then she will open her present on that lucky day, and even if she doesn't, it's kinda same for him since he has no way of contacting her. He must wait till the vacations are over to know everything if she decides to tell him honestly that is.

Enjoying every bit of time as a child, the days went by and now he finds himself sweaty, sweaty in this shivery morning. He's been doing nothing, yet he feels hot and breathless, heart thumping like he's been running for hours. This is the day he was waiting for so long; this is the day he kept nagging his father to stay in Nainital for another

2 weeks, this is the day he feels happiness beyond measure and this is the day he feels anxious. *When will she open the gift cover? Has she opened it yet? Or did she see what's inside days before today? Did she like it, or should I say will she like it? Ugh! What's happening? It's so frustrating! I can't ask her, I can't check up on her, what is this era? Are we living in Stone Age or something? I can't even write her letters. One, I don't have her address. Two, I don't know if she's the one receiving and opening it, alone, especially alone. Oh, I wish there was a way, some way, to let me know about her this instant.*

It is her birthday, and with no means of contacting her, all he can do is imagine her cute reactions as her hands pull out the wrap to reveal the book, the way she reacted last time.

Back when they were in the honeymoon period of their dating life, Shivansh had had everything planned out days before her birth month, not her birthday. Day and night he kept brainstorming about a "perfect" gift for her, he kept asking his male friends, female friends, single friends and the rare, committed friends. The problem was he couldn't come up with anything new or special, that would make her feel special. There were two things he knew she wanted but he had already gifted those things to her when they met for the first time. He's been always like this, not leaving anything for the future, just giving everything he has to offer without holding back.

It took him 10 days to finally decide on something, a letter. Of course, what could best the letter for a couple of old schools? He did write some lines for her often but never a letter, and there couldn't be a better opportunity. With no hesitation, he went to the nearest store to buy some coloured pens, high-quality paper and an envelope.

He puts everything aside on his desk and starts collecting the perfect words to scrape up perfect sentences to brew a perfect letter. It kept him up all night, but he couldn't finish it, work seemed a whole lot tougher than usual that day, maybe it was because of his lack of sleep or maybe it was because of him waiting to go back and continue writing. It's not usual but some people can take their time writing letters, he took three, three days. He was ready to finally post it but, there's always a but, he didn't know her address and no way in hell was he gonna ask her about it.

Then Kavya came to rescue, her younger sister. They both knew each other, after Shivansh and Shweta started dating, and often recommended each other movies and shows only to get added to their watchlists, and sometimes watched too. He asked her for a favour, she said no. It was not like she didn't want to help him; it was just too hard to fetch a letter in the same house without letting the other one notice.

She asked him to ask Shweta's friends to help him out, but he already did. One of them was out of town and the other lived too far from her, it would be impossible to reach her in case of snowfall. So, all he could rely on was Kavya, she knew it would be a formidable task to get the letter and keep it hidden from Shweta, but she agreed to take it on after she tried to ask some of her friends and getting rejected.

He asked her if she had a long-distance friend with whom she was still in touch, and her family knew about her too. And yes, there was one. Ideally, the story would unfold like this: Kavya gets the letter from the post office instead of waiting for them to deliver it home and hides it somewhere where Shweta cannot find it, hopefully. If anything goes off the rails, no one (again, hopefully) would think it is suspicious for Kavya to receive a letter from her friend Divya. Maybe Divya wants to send her a birthday card on her birthday which is just a week before from Shweta's birthday, on Christmas.

The perfect letter had a perfect plan to reach the birthday girl at the perfect time. All he was left to do was to write it again neatly with his newly bought coloured pencils, a boy could do anything to see his girl happy, putting it in the envelope and sending it. Something good happened while he was struggling with his letter, he came up with another idea.

A photograph! *Yes! That would just complete it,* he thought. He grabbed his phone and opened the favourites section in his gallery. It was filled with her photos; one could not tell if it was his phone or her. He began to select the cutest pics to finally select the best one among them. Another half an hour later, he was left with more than 50 photos. It was impossible now to choose one. *What now? Ugh! Why is this so hard? I need to get this done soon else it may not reach on time. Wait… what if I just use all these photos? What if I choose a single portrait and make a mosaic? Yes! That's it! Shivansh, you are a genius, an unprecedented genius!*

He then looked for a photo, worthy enough to be the central figure and truly express her personality. *Yes, this is the one. The way she's sitting, the way she's holding her chin high, shining in confidence she has in herself and her eyes, her eyes showing the purity of her soul. One can talk so much about her just by getting a glance at this pic. And I can't be more grateful for the location she chose, that slightly wet-looking well-maintained green grass and spotless blue sky behind her. She is looking so beautiful. Yes, this is the one.*

Another two hours were gone while he was making the mosaic. Finally, he was again ready to post the letter, he just needed to print that one photo and send it, but it was 1 a.m. Again, he couldn't get the job done and had to wait for the next day to arrive. Regardless of time, he called Majnu.

'Hel... Hello?' he replies in his sleep.

'Hello, Majnu bhaiya. Shivansh this side'

'Why'd you call in the middle of the night sir? I am sleeping, is anything urgent?'

'Yes bhaiya, it is an urgent matter. I have to get a photo printed in A5 size by tomorrow evening'

'Sir please come in the morning; I'll give it to you in the evening'

'Bhaiya please don't hang up, I've to go to work in the morning I might not be able to come. I'll send you the photo and I'll come and get it in the evening. Please, don't forget bhaiya it's really important.'

'Okay sir I'll do it' and he hung up the phone.

Shivansh composed a mail with the subject "URGENT! PRINT THIS PHOTO IN BEST QUALITY" and clicked the attachment icon to select the photo he worked on. He was about to select the most recent photo but his attention went to another photograph. This one was taken by her friend, both were looking at her, but she was standing at a higher ground with sun on the back. It was impossible to look at the camera directly so, they both covered their faces with their hand and kept smiling or rather laughing at the genius photographer who thought the angle would be "cute" for a picture. *Indeed, the angle was the cutest among all.* He thought, looking at his favourite photo of them. He selected that one as well and hit send.

The next day he called Majnu again a 11 to remind him to print the photos.

'Yes sir, I have it ready with me. That's the first thing I did in the morning. You both are such a lovely couple, *Nazar na lage apko*'

'Thank you bhaiya, I'll get it by lunch time. And sorry for waking you up so late last night.'

'No problem, sir'

After work, he went straight to Majnu and looked at the photos. A broad smile covered his face as the photos looked even better than he had imagined. He then folded the two-page letter around the photos carefully in a manner that they fit in the envelope like a glove and rushed to the post office.

December 4th, he posted the letter. Kavya received it on the 14th of December, four days before the day. He was hoping for it to get delivered by the 16th or 17th of December but to his surprise when he checked his phone after lunch, he felt a great relief to finally see his letter in Kavya's hand.

The weird feeling in his stomach was gone. All he was left to do was to wait for the day to come and avoid any slip of the tongue in front of Shweta. He was careful not to mention anything close to her birthday, not even her birthday. He had hoped that Kavya wouldn't spill the beans.

The problem was, she did. Apparently, she wasn't as clever and secretive as he had hoped her to be. Nevertheless, Shweta continued to act clueless, though she knew only about the letter.

It was the night of 17th December, the clock struck midnight and unlike any other boyfriend, Shivansh was not calling Shweta but waiting for her to finish talking to her parents and then getting surprised by Kavya. Kavya had already wished her, and when she was on the phone, receiving more calls from her friends that would not be answered anytime soon, many text notifications started coming and she got frustrated. She activated DND and continued to talk in peace.

Kavya grabbed the opportunity to sneak into the other room and get the letter for her. She came back and waited for her to hang up. Shivansh was staring at the screen, expecting the call any moment. She hung up the phone and Kavya gave her the surprise she already knew about, Shweta being Shweta, preferred knowing about the surprises over getting surprised out of the blue. Just like always, she carefully started to tear the envelope as if not to hurt it. While sliding the letter out of it one photograph slipped and fell on her lap. "This is my favourite photo of us" were the words on the back. She looked at it for a couple of seconds then curiosity got the better of her and she opened the letter only to find another photograph. "This is my favourite photo of you", this photo was a little different. It was not just a photo, but it had many of their photos stitched together to make a wonderful mosaic, containing some of her best memories, with him, some of them without him, and some were of her making cute and funny faces. She tried to see each little picture in it that he had spent hours placing one by one.

HAPPY BIRTHDAY PRINCESS!

As I put my pen on this insignificant piece of paper, I try to convey all my ineffable feelings of mine through some words to the best of my capability.

So, the first thing being the most obvious one, An extremely joyful birthday to you! The moment you are reading this and the moment I was writing this is different, but I feel the same nevertheless, if not more. I just want to come flying to you and kiss all over your face again and again and again! I want to hold you so tight and for so long that we forget everything including the passage of time. I hope you are at least just as happy as me because I am, at this instant, the happiest man alive. Today, I feel happier than I do on my own birthday, I feel like those guys in fairytales, born in the same universe and timeline, destined to find you.

Not that you need someone to support you as you are much stronger than you know but you will always find me by your side even if the world turns against you. Not in front of you protecting but by your side, holding hands, facing anything and everything that comes your way. If you feel low, even for a moment, just repeat these lines in your head and you'll get through anything.

"You are the best, most beautiful, gorgeous and smart. You can face anything."

And always remember even if the world stops revolving around you I won't.

Those days we spent together for the first time were the best days of my life. I got to see your face, listen to your soothing voice, touch your hands and feel your warmth, and your laugh, is that even legal? I literally get zoned out when you laugh, trust me it can get pretty dangerous. You know that I say that I don't feel as much as others do but when I saw you leave, I felt like a part of my heart was getting ripped out. I miss you so much every passing moment. I wish I never had to leave you.

Shweta, you are the best decision I made. You changed the world for me and the way I see life. I just want to take a moment to thank your parents that they made you and raised the way they did. I want to thank every idiot who could've had a chance to be with you but didn't, only to lead you to my arms.

I think you are the soulmate that I never believed existed for me. I love you so much, you are the love of my life and I cannot love anyone, ever, the way I love you.

-Forever yours

AND AGAIN
HAPPY BIRTHDAY!

He gave her a call right after she was done reading the letter and staring at the photos, Kavya helped him with the timing. The phone had hardly rung even for a second when she picked up.

'Happy birthday princess!!'

'Thank you…' she replied smiling.

'So, how was your surprise? Wasn't expecting this, right?' he said in pride.

'Ummm, I don't want to ruin it for you but I kinda I knew about it, about the letter. Photos were definitely something I wasn't expecting.'

'What! Really?' he was shocked, who wouldn't be after doing everything he could and failing to hide a surprise from the one it was meant for?

'Yeah…'

'But how did you find out? And since when?'

'One, Kavya was being too nice which never happens and by never, I mean never, and offered to go to the post office herself and hand over the monthly instalment with her own hands. She has never done that. Two, of course, I know you, I mean how could you not do something like this? Heck, I was worried that you might do something so grand that could give me a little heart attack or something. You couldn't only wish me and do nothing. I know you Mr.'

'Okay, I'll take that as a compliment. And Kavya, she was so confident, even I got carried away and thought she was doing everything perfectly. She's so stupid!' he said with an unavoidable blush from the way she said she knew him, in and out.

'But you know what, I liked it. I mean I prefer knowing rather than getting surprised and not knowing how to react. If I didn't know about this then I'd be worrying about what you might do and getting unnecessarily stressed over it. I knew it about the letter so, I was at peace.'

'Wouldn't you be happier if you were still mad at me and knew nothing about my plan, and then getting surprised all of a sudden?'

'No, If I were mad at you and received it, then my mood would have only shifted to neutral but as you know now, I was happy knowing about it and only got happier after getting your present. What would you choose from mad to neutral or happy to happier?'

'Okay, whatever you say madam. I don't get it but I think it's all good, and seriously asking, did you or did you not like it?'

'Yes, of course, I loved it! I could almost relate to every part of it especially when you wrote about our first date and when the time came to go back to our ways. I too wish that we had more time.'

'Yeah, that was pretty hard to accept. Despite that, I went back smiling. My friend was calling me the whole day to know what was going on and the moment you disappeared from my eyes I started to register that I wasn't feeling quite okay about you going away, he called again. I picked up and got bombarded with his questions.

"Forgot your friend for your girl huh? How was it? What did you guys do? Where did you go? What was she like? Tell me everything!" I said, "Stop, let me speak first." Then I started telling him about our day while going back. Before I knew it, I was in my room, packing and ready to leave and still talking to that idiot.'

'What did you tell him? Did you tell him everything? You better did not.'

'Of course, I didn't, I know what to say and what to skip. Leaving that, tell me about the photos. Did you like them? Are you getting them framed or something? Will they be sitting on your desk?'

'Sure, I'll keep them where everyone can see them. And God knows what will happen to me when mom and dad see them'

'What about your photo? That should be acceptable I think…'

'It would have been perfectly okay if it didn't have photos of us together…'

'Yeah… I should have chosen your portraits only… But I think it came out pretty good, didn't it? Those photos contain such sweet memories now.'

'Yeah, these are lovely. Look at the time now, we've been talking for so long you have to go to work!'

'And so do you…' he says hinting that he is not going to sleep anytime soon.

'I have college! I can manage. Nobody asking anything I'm not there, but you have to go, you can't just skip work, can you?'

'I'll manage…'

'No, you won't! And I'm quite tired, I too need to sleep now.'

'You are saying this just to make me sleep, I know'

'Whatever, just go now! Good night. *I love you*' she whispers at the end.

'Okay fine, good night. I love you and again, happy birthday!'

'Thank you so much'

They both slept that day with an unusually broader smile. Shivansh was finally relieved that she received her present the way he wanted. Kavya did mess up a little but that too ended up better in a way.

He woke up late that day and like she told him he couldn't just leave work. He got tempted for a second to call in sick, but he survived through and made himself get up and leave for work, getting late he forgot to take his phone with him. Lack of sleep made him look ill so; it wasn't hard convincing his boss to leave early. The first thing he did when he reached his room was to pick up his phone and speed dial her contact.

'How's the day going for the birthday girl?' he asked.

'It is quite a day, woke up super late then skipped college. Talked to Mom and Dad again in the morning. Dad wrote such a lovely message for me in his *status*; it made my day. It's the best gift I got! I miss both of them so much today.'

'Of course, he got the first place, I hope I'm second... by the way, you outside?'

'Yeah, I'm out with my cousins. Getting the cake and other stuff...'

'Oh, you are doing birthday shopping. That's great! And I know you can't talk much right now so; I'll be waiting for your call.'

'Okay then, see ya'

'Yup, see you.'

Later that day he came up with another cute plan for her. He gave her a call at 11 and talked for about an hour. It was 11:56 pm when he said, 'Listen, I know people who care about you, your parents, your friends had the first right to wish you so, I didn't wish you first. Also, I didn't want to rush that precious moment when you were opening your present and us talking without worrying that someone else might call. But I can be the last one to wish you and give you a tiny present so, listen carefully to what I am about to say as I am not gonna repeat myself, this is so embarrassing.'

He took some time gathering up the courage to survive the embarrassment and remember the lines and said,

'*Ek ladki dekhi, bilkul bijli ki tarah...*

One flash, ek chamak or mai apna dil kho baitha

Mujhe lagta hai mujhe uss ladki se pyar ho gaya hai

Bas, ab ek hi tamanna hai, rehna hai uske dil me,

Rehna h tere dil me...'

He stopped speaking, waiting for her to say something. Shweta was finding it difficult to believe what she had just heard. She could remember faintly the day when she told him about the dialogue from the movie, *Rehna hai tere dil me*, and how she loved that dialogue. It became her dream to hear those words from a boy. Little did she know was those words she said so unassumingly, had enchanted Shivansh so deeply that he couldn't forget about it even if he wanted to. It was hard for her to believe that he chose such a perfect time to breathe life into her silly dream.

Being the "master" of words, all she could say was, 'You remembered this...?'

'Well, yes. I looked it up on the internet and rehearsed it a million times and it was pretty hard but think I nailed it, didn't I? Anyway, the time is 11:59 pm now so, Happy birthday Shweta! I think nobody can steal my spot to be the last one to wish you now. I wanted to make you feel special, even more than every other day and you have no idea what I wanted to do, or what I could have done for you, but I know you don't like grand gestures, so I had to rein in all my ideas. I hope I did make you feel special...'

'Shivansh, you are so stupid! Of course, you made me feel special for a thousandth time, you always do. In fact, you make me happy.'

These last four words have been in his mind ever since he heard them for the very first time. These words make him keep going. He is dying to hear these words again from her in this life.

After doing everything he could, not being able to contact her was quite the task. He can only wait now, for the vacation to end, *never had*

I thought that the day would come when I wait and wish for the vacation to end, for her to stand next to him.

Shweta, more than 800 kilometres away from Shivansh, somehow managed to suppress her desire to open the present till today. No more waiting, she can now find a spot and open it alone as she knows she might find another note waiting for her inside it.

After getting showered with love and blessings from everyone in the family, she is now alone in her room holding a book covered in a gift wrap in her short arms. She brings it in front of her face, and wonders which book she might find in the next few seconds, which story she might find to get lost in. Turning the book around in all directions she tries to find the ends of the wrap to open it neatly. Pulling some tapes from the right place makes it easier to open the wrap unharmed.

Delight, her face cannot hide what goes in her head. Her tiny fingers glide across the title, The Fault in Our Stars, she wants to see him right now but that cannot happen. Like him, she has to go through each day of the vacation waiting for the school to open, probably the only two children in the school. She can remember the time when he mentioned the book, in one of the early meetings with him and that made her consider buying that novel but receiving it like this, on her birthday, certainly sends butterflies in her stomach. There is nothing else in the world she wants to do but to start reading this right now. The torment she went through for the last couple of days is now over.

She opens the book. *That idiot! I knew he would do something like this.* Another note from him.

Hey birthday girl,

I think it might be the right time to say so, Happy birthday Shweta! I believe you are opening this on your birthday, thank you for being so patient, you really are a polite girl. I knew you could do it.

I hope you are in good health and everyone in your family is overjoyed about your birthday. I think you barely managed some time to have a look at my present because nobody is leaving you even for a moment. Wear a cute dress tonight, invite all your good friends and have a blast! If

> you want, I can try to be there on your next birthday but no promises.
>
> The Shweta I know would have read the novel way before the end of the vacation and would tell me just how much she loved it. I miss the school, my friends and you. See you soon.
>
> -Shivansh

Shivansh on the other side, is spending his day wondering about her. *I wish I could wish her, see her open the present, the smile that comes afterwards, the redness of her cheeks and ears, her tucking her hair behind her ear...* Walking back and forth, staring at the ceiling and not listening to anyone around him the first time they call him, that's how his day is going.

'Beta, come down and serve tea to the guests' Pooja shouts for the third time, slightly annoyed.

'Yes maa, I'll be there in a minute' he says nicely, controlling his frustration.

Runs to the kitchen through the stairs, gets a scolding from Pooja who is already angry at him, takes the tray and goes to the guests. Coming back, he can hear his father's phone ringing, but he ignores it even knowing that he can't leave the guests to receive the call.

'Beta, take a look at the phone, you know your father is with guests' says Pooja from the kitchen.

He rolls his eyes and goes to pick up the phone. *The elder brother has to do all the work, doesn't he?*

It is a call from an unknown number, he wonders if he should answer the call or not but does anyway.

'Hello...' he says hoping that the person on the other side might give an introduction first.

'Shivansh?' comes a sweet girly voice from the phone.

It takes only an instant to turn his mood 180 degrees. How can he not recognize the voice he was hoping to hear the most since the past few days?

'Happy birthday Shweta!' he whispers. 'Maa, it's my friend, he's asking something about the homework.' He shouts on his way out.

'Thank you so much for the gift, I can't even imagine the trouble you went through to manage all of this.' She says in excitement which makes him feel happiness beyond measure.

'It was not trouble for me. I wanted to do that, and it wasn't even that hard. Been saving my pocket money for quite a while' he replies trying to act as manly as possible. 'And come to think of it, I don't remember sharing my dad's contact with you. Seems like there was someone else going through trouble.'

'It was not trouble for me' she replies, mimicking Shivansh and they both burst into laughter. Pooja hears him laughing and asks what it is about.

'Nothing maa, told you it's my friend. He made a blunder with his homework, I'll come and tell you in a minute.' Then getting back on the call, 'Seriously, please tell me you didn't break into the school and stole my contact by hacking the school records' they laugh again, louder this time. Shivansh controls his laugh, partly because his mom will not like it and mostly because he wants to listen to her laugh, he loves the way she laughs, not covering her face, not suppressing her voice, not acting politely, completely freely.

'I just... I just asked... Aakash, stupid!' she tries to speak in between her laugh.

'Oh... okay. So, tell me how's your day going? Who's coming to the party?'

'Day's been great so far. I'm quite the centre of attention today and I'm loving this treatment. About the party, not many, just a couple of close friends are coming. Maybe some of my family friends too.'

'You are always my centre of attention. I hope you love that too.'

Silence. She doesn't know what to say to that.

'Anyway, tell me how's everyone at home? What gifts did you get from whom?' he tries to get her out of that awkward situation.

'Umm... yeah, everyone's great. No gifts as of now, maybe later. You tell me how's everyone there and your cute little brother, what's he doing? How much are you enjoying your vacation back in your hometown? Your Grandparents must be happy to see you.'

'Woah! So many questions! Well, everyone's doing great, my *cute little brother* is busy playing, free from all the care in the world. The vacation's been fine for me, nothing too exciting but nothing too boring either. And yes, they are happy to have their grandkids back at home. It is so cold over here, how are you surviving there? And how are your holidays going?'

'Yes, it is freezing! I so want to skip the winters. Every day's quite boring, especially from now on. At least I had this huge anticipation about the present, even that is gone now.'

'But you have a novel now that must make up for some days...'

'Two days... maybe three at max, if I don't start reading it today.'

'Well, if I had more money, I could've packed some more...'

'Oh c'mon, doing this was more than enough. Thank you for such a lovely and thoughtful gift!'

'I'll take that as you liked it... Am I right?'

'Yes, I did. Rest I'll let you know once I read it. I was trying to get it either by saving or asking

Dad since it was so highly recommended by you, claiming that I'm gonna love it.'

'That, you will!' he says with his usual over-the-top confidence.

'Where do you get that?'

'Where do I get what?'

'That overconfidence!'

'Oh that, I was born with it'

'Yeah, sure!' They both laugh a little more.

'Don't forget to tell me when you've read it.'

'Sure, and Shivansh, Thank you for this. It really made my day better by a mile.'

'Well, if it made you happy then I have done good enough, I guess. Again, happy birthday Shweta, have loads of fun today and the rest of the holidays. See you at School.'

'See ya.'

It gets hard to go in front of anyone after hanging up the phone, they cannot make their smile go away, and they cannot tone down their blush. *Is it her birthday or mine? Getting surprised like that, I could have never expected a phone call from her. I think I got a bigger surprise than her. Whatever, this was great. Everything was great!* She saved him from the agony he could have faced not knowing about her feelings when she opened the present. He is so happy now that he can serve tea a thousand times without any complaint.

Shweta is now ready to go out with her father to get something for her. She cannot think of a better birthday than today except if he could have come and given her the gift, in her hands, and enjoyed her party, with her.

Shivansh asks his mother to make something sweet, like kheer, tonight. Pooja agrees. In the evening, he thinks, *only if I could share this kheer with her.* And Shweta wonders if there's a chance to see him tonight.

In the end, they both go to bed wishing for a little more.

CHAPTER 09:
WHAT TOOK YOU SO LONG?

Two years have passed since Shivansh started his new life and now his life is completely different from what he had lived for the first time, it is so different that he can no longer predict anything, he no longer knows everything, it's like he's living for the first time and all he went through was just a bad dream.

Shivansh and Shweta have grown closer, close enough to be called a couple by everyone, all the time. They cannot spend a moment without each other, yet they haven't confessed their feelings to each other. Continuing to brush off people whenever they try to drag them into the discussion.

'When are you going to confess to her, don't you think you've waited for too long? I mean practically everyone knows you both are in love. I'm not saying go and tell her right now, but I think you should think about it and do something soon...' says Aakash suddenly in the middle of an idle talk.

Knowing what's the right thing to do and actually having the courage to do so are completely different things, even more so when the right thing to do is confessing your love. Cmon Shivansh! You know Aakash is right. Haven't you done this already? You can do it! And you know she likes you; she told you that she did, back in the school days, didn't she? And by the tremendous time you spend together, there's no doubt. It's been two years; remember you will be going soon if you don't do it now then you might have to do it like that again. Don't you want to stand next to her and tell her how much you love her? Don't you want to escape from this situation? Aren't you tired of holding back your feelings for so long? How long are you going to wait for? How long are you going to make her wait? Look, she's coming. She is going to say something to you. Just tell her that you love her right now! Shivansh, you got this.

'Hey!' she says in her tender voice which makes his heart melt every day.

'Shivansh! I know you heard her, you need to give her a reply...' Aakash shakes him to bring him back from his thoughts.

'Hey, good morning.' He says, smiling awkwardly.

Look at him! He's so cute. Smiling with that awkwardness, he must be wondering what happened. I don't know where he gets lost sometimes. 'Good morning, any plans for tomorrow? My usual, no plans...'

'Actually, I do have something in mind. *I want to tell you what you already might know.* I want to show you something nice and I'm not going to tell you what it's going to be, of course, but you are coming with me, no questions.'

'You are always like this. What's it gonna be this time...?'

'You'll get know...' he says, as always.

'Ugh! I know I can't get it out of you no matter how much I try. So, I will not even try. Let's see what you come up with.'

'Great! I'll tell you the details later.'

'Sure, let me know.'

The usual conversation killer for them, the next teacher, arrives and she goes to her seat.

Sunday evening, the evening that is going to be so special for him, the evening he is going to tell her about his feelings, the evening before the day they start dating. He has looked all over the internet to decide what to wear and come up with an outfit with the clothes he has. Carefully making the choices to look neither overdressed nor completely casual. Ready, he takes some of his saved pocket money and goes to the regular spot where they meet. He sees her coming, looking as gorgeous as always if not more. *I didn't ask her to wear something nice or anything. Why is she wearing that dress? Does she already know?*

'Hey!' she says with the same cute smile she wore the previous day.

'Hey, you came dressed…'

'Says who.'

'What? These are my daily clothes, aren't they?'

'And so are mine.'

'Okay, here take this.' He hands her a chocolate.

'Why do you always do this?'

'You don't like chocolates?'

'I do. You know that's not what I'm talking about.'

'So, you don't like me bringing chocolates for you?'

'Ugh! No, that's not… But why always?'

'Stop it.' He laughs a little. 'We won't go anywhere like this. Remember I have something to show you? Now follow me.'

'And what is that?'

'Just come with me.'

'All right let's go…'

They have been walking for more than 10 minutes, she can now tell that they are not going to some shop, she knows what's going on.

'Don't tell me you found another place for sunset viewing…'

'I did. I found it a long time ago.'

'Then why didn't you show me sooner?'

'That's because…' *woah I was about to say it,* 'that place is quite far. We can't just go there whenever we want, it needs some planning and time.'

'Still, you found another spot. God knows how many have you discovered.'

'Now don't go saying "You should try being a guide or something." Okay?'

'That's exactly what I was about to say! How do you do this? Always!'

'I just know you. Now stop talking and follow me. This is gonna get some hard work and you don't have much stamina either.'

She is following Shivansh as he asked her to. The path has now become narrower, it is not even a road anymore. They are walking on a trail, on the left they can see the houses on distant mountains, on the right, there are all kinds of trees, mostly Deodar. They can feel the strong breeze coming from the left, her hair keeps her busy, and her cheeks are slightly redder than they already were. She's tired. Complaining continuously, she keeps asking how far is this place, and he keeps telling her "Just a few steps away".

After some weary 30 minutes, crossing the trail, rarely used by the villagers they are here, at the edge of a mountain. Lake is visible from here, with almost no mountain behind it. Indeed, a lovely view, the wind is stronger here, hitting right into their faces and passing through the tree leaves to make sounds close to musical notes in harmony, simultaneously making the trees dance in sync with the music nature is trying to play.

Since she is quite tired, she sits and looks at him, waiting for him to say something. Little does she know that he's about to say something that is not anywhere near her expectations. The sun is also tired, like her cheeks it turns red as it moves closer to the lake, making the lake and clouds above it turn to gold.

'Great, isn't it?' he looks at Shweta hoping to hear that it is great, and it was worth walking all the way here.

'It is, it is beautiful, maybe the best in all Nainital. How is it still not known; I don't think any tourists come here either.'

'What you think is right Ms Shweta, I'm not sure if there are people other than me that know this place. Anyway, let's just sit here for a while, we arrived at the perfect time. What are about to see might be the most beautiful sunset of your life.'

The sun is kneeling, about to kiss the lake, there cannot be a more perfect moment for him to tell her what he's been holding only to himself for so long.

His pulse starts to rise higher than it has ever been, blood runs up his cheeks, his ears turn redder than chilli flakes, and he wipes his face twice before he tries to speak. He opens his mouth, but no words come out, his throat is drying up, and his legs stopped listening to him long ago. *What's happening all of a sudden? I don't think I can speak without fumbling.* He gulps, still dry, and takes a second to take out a piece of paper from his pocket and hands it to Shweta without any notice.

'Don't you dare laugh! Just read it.' He manages to bring his voice out, loud yet calm.

'What is this?'

'Just read it, no questions.'

Okay, fine!' she rolls her eyes and flips the page open, revealing his handwriting.

'Did you write?'

Shivansh stares at her, giving her a silent scolding. She gets back to the page and starts reading.

Who is this girl?
How do I know her?

Past all the ungovernable and unfathomable
She barged in
Breaking all my rationalisation
And all my hate for so-called love

Made me do things I thought I never would
Made me the most unreasonable person I could think of

When did my heart become more than just a pump?
Since when did this smile get stuck on my face
And why, for the first time I think
This girl is the one I can't not think about

Am I becoming someone else?
Or just more of myself
Am I really falling for this stubborn dumb girl,
Or is it just a dream?

> Even if it is, I want to sleep more
> Just a little more
> To your eternity
>
> Yours! You cute little clumsy girl!
> You are the answer to my first question;
> And the rest of all the ones I have.

She reads the last line and loses the ability to turn her face back up and look into his eyes. Tears, as fast as they come, drop on the page and she wipes it with her hands, holds it behind her and covers her face with her other hand. Her eyes, her nose, her cheeks, her ears, and the clouds, all look like peach. She starts reading it again, twice and thrice.

For a moment her brain stopped, and now it goes in full throttle. *Is this what I think this is? First of all, What Do I think? Am I even thinking or is this something out of the definition of thinking? Does he like me? Of course, he likes me, but does he like me that way? Wait, did he just confess to me? What am I supposed to say now? Do I like him? Of course, I LOVE him! What took him so long? What took him so long to tell me? Wait, I haven't spoken anything for quite some time. Do I need to say something back to him? I can't stop my tears! This is the worst! I can't look him in the eyes, he will think I'm ugly. Should I say something now? Yes, no, yes, wait no! I think he knows how I feel about him, I don't need to tell him, he always behaves like he knows everything anyway. Yes, he does know, else why would I go so far by a walk that took about an hour if it wasn't for him? Yes, I don't need to say it out loud. It's all right. Wait, why is he not saying anything? He just handed over me this paper and asked me to read it, and I did. So, what is he waiting for? Why isn't he doing anything, or going anywhere? I can't look up right now, I can see his feet, he is looking at me. He's not moving. Is he expecting something from me? Wait, what if it isn't what I think it is? Maybe, he's just showing off his talent, showing me that he can write. Maybe, he wrote it for somebody else, like it happened in "Kuchh Kuchh hota Hai". Am I Anjali in this situation? I wish this is for me, only me. God! Help me!*

'So…?' he can't remember the words he practised for hours in his room. No wonder he came with a paper.

'Did you write this yourself?'

She can see him, standing in front of her. Hands in his pockets, his eyes looking into her eyes with the hope to hear her say something, anything, with slight redness in his cheeks he says, 'Shweta, I love you. You dumbo! And yes, I did write that, for you!' and looks away from her.

He cannot look at her anymore, no matter how much he tries. His eyes avert on their own whenever he tries. With all his strength, he has told her, and now all he wants is to hear her voice and tell him what he's been dying to hear.

Shweta starts laughing, she can't stop. It's not like she finds this funny, but it just came naturally. She's happy, beyond happy, she just got confessed to by her crush, her first crush. Her soft giggles have something magical that takes Shivansh somewhere else, like some people get lost in the music, her laugh is his favourite place to get lost in. He can never get enough of her laugh, especially today because she's laughing exactly like she did when he confessed to her last time, like he promised that he would make it up to her.

It happened on the 14th of August, the Independence Day of our little neighbouring nation, the way they remembered this day. In the last exam of her third semester, she was going to meet with one of her two best friends, Tanya.

Since he was too busy with a new project, he couldn't come up with a plan to do anything about confessing to her the right way. It was on 13th when he got some free time to think about a way and do something if she agrees to go with his plan. Since they both were huge MCU fans, whenever one of them watched a show or a movie or whenever a new movie was about to come out, they used to have a discussion, sort of.

He texted her. While waiting for her to respond he brainstormed as many ideas as he could, it was hard, to select a perfect way to confess to her without any grand gestures that she hated and found impossible to handle but he could not go too bland either. She didn't text for two hours; it was enough time for him to come up with something that was somewhere between overwhelming and uninteresting. His impatience grew a thousand-fold when he had figured out almost everything but still didn't hear from Tanya. He waited and waited but no reply from her. The time was passing away, if he didn't get to talk to her on time then it'd be too late, and he would not get another chance like this one again. He texted her again, "Text me back ASAP whenever you see this, it's urgent!" He then shifted his focus to something that he could do on his own. Another hour passed, and he had prepared something, but it was incomplete if he couldn't get to talk to her, it was becoming harder and harder to wait. There was nothing more he could do.

The torment took a halt when he received a text from Shweta. It was hard to keep his emotions under check, he tried his best not to let her know anything, to behave the way he usually does. They couldn't talk for long, after all, she to prepare for her last exam. She kept saying she had so much to cover, and she had not nearly enough time to do that.

Shivansh, for a change, agreed and asked her to go back to her books in exchange for extra time the next day. *I hope she doesn't find it unusual that I agreed so readily.* Since she had a lot to think about the night before her exam, she didn't want to add up another thing running on her mind. She started studying and he started waiting for her friend's text. Time wasn't very kind to him, he had to do something while waiting for an unknown period of time. He dialled up his friend's number.

'Listen, I can't come tomorrow. Make something up like I've got a fever or something, anything, just make sure nobody calls me tomorrow. I'll leave it to you.'

'Wait, what happened? You good?'

'Yes, I am perfectly fine. You don't need to worry. I'll tell you the details later. Can you do that?'

'Okay, I'll handle that, but you owe me a treat then. Beer party would be just fine.'

'All right, done. Thanks, man.'

'Mention not.'

Another problem was solved. Since most of the work was done, he didn't need to be at work as much and the day after that is Sunday so, no worries there.

2 am, he slept with no reply from her. He woke up late the next morning, Shweta was already outside the gate, waiting for it to open so

she could go for her exam. She told him how she woke up on time but still managed to get late and barely caught the last bus to reach there. Shivansh kept checking his phone while talking to her, but her friend still hadn't replied. Shweta went to take her exam. All he was left with was to wait till the exam was over and somehow tell her how much he liked her without any help from her friends. But, for once, when he had lost all hope, he saw a notification blink on his phone, it was a text from Tanya. He started typing the moment he unlocked his phone.

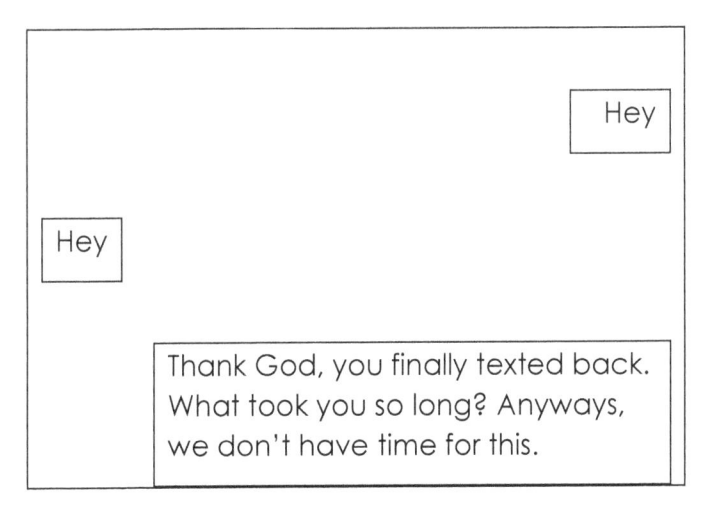

> Hey

> Hey

> Thank God, you finally texted back. What took you so long? Anyways, we don't have time for this.

> Listen, Tanya, the thing is I want to confess my feelings to her, and I want you to help me. She must have told you what happened last time. I want to fix that, and I have a plan.
>
> You on board?

Shivansh, actually the thing is something urgent came up and I had to come to my college and I have no idea how long it'll take for me to get free. I haven't even told Shweta that I won't be able to meet her after her exam.

> Okay. I'll figure something out then. Bye.

With all of his plans crumbling down, Shivansh thought it was all his fault for not planning this through, if he had started working on it in time then he could've worked something out, but it was too late. Improvising at the last moment could only take him so far, he had only one chance and that was gone. He was still a step away from accepting his defeat, still trying to figure something out, a way to make it happen, something, anything that could work.

What is it now? He thought in frustration, he wanted to have some peace so he could think of something when he saw his phone screen lit up. Another text from Tanya gave him another ray of hope. It was the contact info of Khushi, her only other best friend. She suggested him to get her help. He had never talked to her, he knew she was not the kind to start talking to someone comfortably, being an introvert. Out of options, he texted her immediately, not expecting much.

> Hey, Khushi. Shivansh this side. I believe Shweta has told you about me...

> Hey, Shivansh. How are you? And yes, she did tell me about you. She didn't tell me that she gave you my contact though.

> I'm good thank you. How are you? And about the contact, she didn't. Tanya did. Khushi, I have a favour to ask.

He then told her everything about the plan, what he wanted her to do, and how he talked to Tanya first, but she couldn't help him, and she was the only person he could rely on. To one of his biggest surprises, she agreed. He thought she was nothing like Shweta described her, she wasn't awkward while talking, and she didn't even hesitate to help him out when she was talking to him for the first time, maybe she was being so helpful to him for Shweta's sake. For him, it was nearly a miracle, something the universe wanted to happen. He couldn't thank her enough. His plan came back to life after nearly taking the last breaths.

Following his lead, she went to a few shops to get a bouquet but not one of them had one. They then decided that she would take the bouquet and chocolates for her on her way to meet her. Meanwhile, Shivansh started making some phone calls.

'Hello, Simz Café?'

'Yes sir, how may I help you?'

'Actually, I have a favour to ask. Can you arrange a bouquet for someone special to me? She's going to visit there in two or three hours.'

'No sir, we can't help you with that.'

'C'mon bro, maybe you can do this on a personal level. I can pay in advance. I don't want anything else like songs or lighting, just a small bouquet. You don't even have to tell your manager about this, just get one from a shop nearby.'

'Sorry sir, I wish I could, but I can't help you with that. We are already short-staffed...'

'Okay...' he hung up the phone, not losing hope, he dialled another number.

'Hello, Blooming Buds?'

'Yes?'

'I want to get a bouquet delivered.'

'Sorry sir, the delivery services are not available today.'

'Can't you make an exception? I am ready to pay some extra amount.'

'No sir, it won't be possible.'

'Hello, Yellow Petals?'

'No sir.'

'Hello, Addy's café?'

'Sorry sir.'

'Café Himalaya?'

'Sorry sir.'

'Becafe? I have a favour to ask...'

'Sorry sir, we cannot help you.'

He tried almost all the flower shops and cafes but the city she lived in did not want to do anything in his favour today. *Why today?* He told Khushi about all the phone calls he made. Even she couldn't believe that there was not a single shop that could do what they wanted. She told him to calm down, there was this last thing that they could try. He asked her to tell him about her idea with his flickering spirit.

'Okay, let's do one thing. I'll go pick her up after the exam and we'll then go to Capital Shopping Complex, a mini shopping mall sort of, it's quite far but I think I can make it work. After that, when I think the time is right, I'll ask her to wait for me and I'll get the things I can find. How's that?'

'I think it's perfect. I really wanted to order the things from here but like I told you it's impossible so, if you can go the extra mile and buy some things for me, I'd really appreciate that.'

'Sure, just tell me what to get, what I do manage to get is a different story altogether.'

'I think a novel would be nice, she loves novels. You must know that better than me. I have two options and it's quite confusing actually. There's this novel that my friend suggested that is great and she hasn't read it and then there's this novel that she has read on her phone and wants to have a hard copy of her own. What do you say?'

'Shivansh, I can't decide… I can try to get whatever you ask me to.'

'Okay then, she hasn't read *The Hating Game* so, I want you to look for this one first and if you can't find this one then go for *The Notebook* and if you can't find that one then I don't think you'll get any decent book from that weird mini-mall. And let's add something to that too, I think you know this one already, a small bouquet. You know she cannot handle anything grand, please get a small one. And a chocolate would be nice, wouldn't it? I think that's it. Now, do I need to send the approximate sum right now or you can buy it first and then tell me the amount so I can send it then?'

'I'll see what I can get. And Shivansh she must have told you that I have a job so, don't worry about that.'

'All right then, tell me the moment you leave her side, the moment you get all the things, and the moment you get back to her.'

'Sure.'

'Wait, one more thing.'

'Yes?'

'I prepared this audio file for her to listen when you hand over the presents to her and I am not sure if she took her earphones with her. So…'

'Yup, I'll take my pair with me and lend her in case she needs it.'

'Thanks a lot!'

'You're welcome.'

Somehow, he was again stuck in the waiting game. He couldn't do anything but to suffer in wait. If he could've ordered something, he would've felt a little less restless but at that moment everything was on her shoulders. He wasn't used to rely on anyone for most of the things so, this was new for him. That uncertainty ate him. A whole hour was left for Shweta's exam to finish. *She must be hyped today, writing in the last exam, and then getting to meet one of her besties after so many days, they swapped I know but still, at least Khushi will be there, that's way better than nobody.*

His phone lit up, he had received two notifications. They were from Tanya, he instantly looked it up. She somehow managed to get out of her college and was going to meet Shweta, as they had planned. Shivansh was delighted to hear this, Shweta would meet both of her besties after the exam, he knows how little they get to meet since they left school and she used to get so overjoyed whenever they planned out to meet. And in disguise, it was good news for him too, he then had two allies instead of one.

It was the beginning of the final act, Shivansh was texting and coordinating with both of them. He was ready to receive Shweta's text anytime and respond accordingly. "She's here, I can see her." Khushi texted, looking from the main gate. His heart grew louder. Shweta was coming out of the hall, towards the front gate. She looked for Khushi beyond the gate, shocked! She found both Khushi and Tanya waiting for her. Her exhaustion left her body, and she became way happier in an instant, a broad smile came on her face. *The happier she is, the better the plan goes,* he thought.

Shweta joined them and started to head for the mini-mall. Shivansh was continuously texting Khushi and Tanya for any changes in the plan or any kind of updates. It was hard for them to text back while Shweta was sitting right next to them, they didn't even text much with anyone that much, to begin with. On their way, Shweta also texted him, freely unlike them.

> Hey, finally I'm free!

> Great! So, when can I find you so we can have a nice, long convo we haven't had in ages?

> I'll text you when I am, rather I'll just call you.

> You waiting for Tanya right now?

> No, I'm with her and guess what? Khushi is here with me too, this is the best day!

> That's great! I don't think I can expect much of your free time while they are with you. Enjoy your time with your besties! And text me when you are free.

> See ya

> Later...

It's so hard to lie to her and act as oblivious as a toddler in front of her. We haven't even talked once on the phone, but tonight we will or maybe sooner than that, if everything goes right that is. Good thing she texted, if she had called me then I would've been exposed instantly. He thought, while checking each and every text he sent her a thousand times. The last thing he wanted to do was to let some hint slip by and let her know about everything, his last chance to make it the perfect confession of love.

He continued to get updates from Khushi and Tanya whenever they could sneak out from Shweta's sharp eyes. They reached the mini-mall, and Khushi let him know. After about five minutes, he unexpectedly received a text from Shweta.

> I did tell you that Khushi and Tanya are only friends through me, right? I mean you know that they aren't that close, don't you?

>> Yes, I know all that. You told me I remember, did something happen?

> I don't know what happened but they are acting weird today. Talking more than usual, talking to each other more than they are talking to me. And aren't

even letting me in in their *discussion*.

> Oh… okay. I get what's going on. They are getting along too well today and someone is getting super jealous. 😆 😆
>
> Try getting in, why are you texting me right now?

They left me. Alone. Can you believe that? Tanya said that she wanted to buy something for her cousin's birthday and took Khushi with her! WTF!

> I think they thought that you must be tired. you had a long day, didn't you? Maybe that's why…

No, they didn't! Something is going on with those two, I know

> it. You know Khushi never hides her phone from me but on our way here, she was texting someone and she was hiding it from me, she didn't even tell me who that was when I asked her straight.

> Maybe she got herself a boyfriend… and if that's true then she'll tell you when she's ready to tell you or maybe she didn't get that perfect chance to tell you. She's not going to tell you about her new boyfriend in a taxi, is she? You told me that she's been busy and It's been so long since you last met.

> Seriously, this day is weird. And why are you taking their side? You should take mine!

> I'm not taking sides, just telling you to calm down and stop overthinking.

> The one thing I cannot do

> Yeah, yeah. Listen, I'm getting a call from Maa. Later...

> Alright, I guess I'll just wait for those two idiots then. Alone!

He found a reasonable way out from Shweta's chat box and started texting Tanya and Khushi. They were now far enough from her to chat freely. They went from shop to shop, talking to Shivansh and telling him whatever they could find.

> So, your cousin's birthday huh, that's some original idea you got there.

It worked okay! How were we supposed to just leave her alone without any kind of excuse? Got any better ideas?? If yes, then you should have told us sooner.

> Alright, it did work. She's not even close to guessing what's about to happen. Great job you two! So, did you find anything?

No, we are still searching. There's no flower shop anywhere in 3-4 km radius.

> And the book...?

We couldn't find *The Hating Game* but we did find *The Notebook*.

> Can you get a big enough chocolate then? Since the bouquet is out of the plan. She Doesn't have any particular preference, I think you can get her anything good.

Sure.

Done! We have everything, we are going back to her, so be ready!

> Alright!! I'm ready, waiting for your signal. Wait! Don't tell her yet, I'll tell you when to. I'm gonna text her first.

Okay.

Shivansh

> Guess what, they came back. Now we'll Have lots n lots of fun!

> Great! But first I'm sending you something, listen to it right now, not later and with the utmost attention. Okay?

> Okayyy

> ▶ audiorecording1.mp3

Shweta was sitting with Tanya and Khushi facing her, she didn't have her earphones with her. After all, it was her exam. Before she could say so Khushi took out her earphones and gave it to her, the moment Shivansh gave her the signal. Shweta was already a little more than just surprised, she sensed that something was about to happen, something big and her friends were also involved in that. She plugged in the earphones and tapped the play button, it was her favourite song "*You Are My Everything"* from a K-drama "*Descendants of the Sun,"* she couldn't not recognise that in the first 2 seconds. But it was only the BGM, no vocals. She got a little confused about the reason he would send something like this and ask her to listen to it then and there. Suddenly, she heard…

♪ 'Hey, Shweta. This is your boyfriend speaking. I know I'm being a little presumptuous, but I am not completely wrong either. You ruined my plan to ask you out properly by asking me to ask you out, with a meme at that! Damn, this is confusing and weird, but our story so far has been pretty weird. From the beginning, let's say different rather than weird.

From you having a crush on me back in middle school to me having a crush on you after all these years spent apart as complete strangers.

Whatever happened was weird, but I look forward to spending some more, way more weird moments with you, only if you say "Yes"! And if your answer is "Yes" then please tell me right now as I'm dying over here for your reply. I so want to listen to your voice, call me right now because Shweta, I like you too much!' 🎵

Tanya and Khushi gave her the book and the chocolate when she was in the middle of listening to his voice note. She was blushing so hard that it was worthless to even try to hide it. Her cheeks gave everything away, she was thunderstruck, and she wasn't even sure what she had heard. She tapped the play button again to listen, to believe what she heard was real. Then she played it again, and again, and again. Finally, with superhuman courage she called Shivansh, for the first time.

Tapping on the floor, Shivansh waited for her, hopefully, call. That day, his bed wasn't the slightest comfy place for him. It wasn't helpful, he went outside and started roaming. Walking almost as fast as someone jogging. Sahil, his friend, saw him and asked him to come and have a chat.

'Later Bisla, not now!' he replied and continued to walk, to avoid more invitations like this.

Sahil being the stubborn one demanded, 'Come here Shivansh, just once!'

Shivansh rolled his eyes, something he had learned from Shweta, and went to Sahil and asked, 'What?'

'Gotta show you this meme real quick' he said as he turned his phone towards him, 'Hilarious, right?'

Poor Shivansh burdened with such suspense, couldn't understand a word from the meme.

'I didn't get it but Bisla, believe me, I'll come back and ask you about it but not now, okay? I have already so much on my plate right now.'

He was about to get up from his bed when his phone lit up with Shweta's name on it. She was calling him! For the first time! He had no idea what to do. *What do you do when someone calls you? You pick up, you pick it up, you idiot! Wait! What are you doing? Don't you think you should get out of here before you answer?*

With a broader smile that his face could barely handle, he left the room in a hurry. The moment he crossed the door, he subconsciously picked up the phone without thinking, he moved his phone close to his ear.

'Hello... Shweta?'

After a short pause, all he could hear was her laugh. She kept laughing, her tone wasn't as if she found something funny but her honest way of laughing, without a doubt, expressed her ecstasy. She couldn't stop, he didn't want her to stop. That soul soothing heart gripping melodious laugh had effortlessly trapped his heart and mind in addictive numbness. All he wanted was to keep prisoned in it, he forgot why she had called him. Getting out of that dopamine rush took some time, he suppressed his desire to keep listening to her voice with superhuman effort and spoke, for the one simple *yes* that could change the course of his life forever.

'Say something, I'm dying for your response over here.'

She continued to laugh for a while and said, 'What?'

'You know what!'

'But you already know it, do I really need to say it?'

'Yes, you do!'

'I can't, I just can't. It's too much for me. My friends are watching me, they are smiling so hard, barely holding back their laughs. You know what I am like, it is too much for me and listening to your voice note here was quite hard. It's too loud and distracting, I heard it twice or thrice, maybe more. I'll go home and listen to it again and then I'll get back to you. Would that be alright?'

'You can say all this, but you can't whisper "I like you too"' he whispered.

'What?' she asked, astounded.

'I like you!' he said, again with a soft whisper.

Shweta couldn't hear him a second time either and said, 'What? Did you just say that you love me?'

Flustered Shivansh had no idea how to say another word to her. After a long pause, he said, 'I said "I like you" rather I asked you to say, "I like you too", got it?' without whispering. 'But it's okay now, enjoy with your friends. You guys have time only till sunset, don't you? Text me when you are free.'

'Okay, see ya pretty boy'

'See you, take care.'

And now, Shweta is laughing the same way she laughed back then, except this time, it is in front of him. All he can do and is doing is wait for her to stop laughing and say what he's been yearning to hear. He adores the way she laughs, looking at her with his arms folded he says nothing.

Shweta notices the way he's been looking at her. She has known him for two years now and sometimes he wears a bittersweet nostalgic look on his face when he looks at her. Whenever she tries to ask him about it, he acts oblivious or ignores her question. Today, he looks the same, she can see him weeping even though he hasn't shed a single drop of water from his eyes. She wants to ask him, for a hundredth time, but she knows how he is going to react if she does so, she just says, 'What? Why are you looking at me like that?'

'Because you are beautiful. I enjoy looking at beautiful people.'

It took so much of her to remain calm in this situation but that one line Shivansh just said was more than enough to get her flustered. Having no idea how it would feel to hear him say that again at this moment, she was defenceless, having read that book made it even more zealous. Leaving her speechless, Shivansh doesn't know what to do next so, he waits for her to say something.

After an uncomfortably long pause, she says, 'What?'

'What do you mean what?'

'What do you want me to do?'

'You know what to do… or what to say… Don't pretend to be so dumb!'

'You know me, you know I cannot say it. It's too much for me to… do you want me to do all the stuff?'

'I know what you can and cannot say, I wrote this whole thing, took you to this place, and even confessed to you and you are saying I want you to do "all the stuff"'

'I didn't say that. Do you have any idea how long I've been waiting? Everyone, literally everyone, thinks that we are dating, even my parents started teasing me by calling me by your name every now and then. But you never said anything. With time, I just accepted the way things were, and I was doing fine but then you suddenly do this…'

'Woah, woah, woah stop! Alright, I get your point but first, don't get your parents and school in this. Second, Yar I wanted to be sure, before I ask you out, about how I feel, about how you feel about me. And why were you waiting for me all this time? You could've just asked me out.'

'No, that's your job!'

'Alright, alright! Now, listen carefully because I don't think I'll be saying this a lot. Shweta, since the day I met you, in fact, the moment I saw you, I've felt something incredible between us and over the last two years, that has only increased stupendously every day. Like you, even I'm tired of telling people that we are just friends because you are more than that to me. Shweta, I am in love with you. Would you be my girlfriend?'

'I love you too, stupid!' tears fill her eyes, she takes a step and hugs him. It is now Shivansh, who is in shock, he feels the same hug he felt years back, the same warmth, the same scent. He can feel her wet cheek touching gently on his, her fragile arms surrounding his neck. He notices his hands moving without his command, holding her by her chin and wiping off her tears. He rests his hand on the back of her head and pulls her towards him, the other hand on her waist. The longer they stay like this, the harder it becomes to let go. To him, it feels like decades have passed since the last time they hugged.

Noticing the cruel passage of time, he feels some pain in his heart, realising it is time to go back home. The surroundings are now wrapped in a completely different palette compared to when they arrived. The hyped pink turned into tired dark orange, greens turned into a colour closer to black. The sun went past the horizon to hide from them, turning the beautiful sunset into the beginning of the night. He summoned all his strength to move his arms to hold her by her shoulders, taking a step back to say against his own will.

'I think we should leave…'

Shweta can feel the pain in his voice, she wants to tell him to stop but she does not. Her eyes get watery again and before she can nod Shivansh pulls her closer, tighter.

It isn't easy but they manage to hold their emotions in check and leave the place before it gets darker. As always, Shivansh goes with her to drop her off at her house. Shivansh cannot let go of her hand; he tries to but fails. Shweta looks at him in a way that reassures him that this isn't the end, they'll meet again the next day. He turns back to hide his face and starts walking, leaving her at her door.

'Shivansh! Where are you going beta? Come and have some sweets, I just made a ton yesterday.' A sweet voice reaches him, and he feels helpless, helpless to deny Shweta's mom, Anjali.

'Namaste Aunty!' he greets her with his hands joined. 'I would love to have some but it's already getting so late, maa will get mad at me if I don't reach soon.'

'Come na beta, don't worry I'll talk to your mother. Okay?'

'Aunty...'

'No more of your excuses, you are coming inside.'

How can one say "no" to that, poor Shivansh goes with the flow. *She's always like this.* They both go inside, he waits for the sweets so he can taste them and leave as soon as possible. Anjali calls Pooja in front of them.

'Hello, Pooja?'

'Hello, Anjali. How are you? Don't tell me Shivansh is there and you called me to defend him.'

'I'm good, how are you? And you are right Shivansh is here, but he didn't get late playing, I asked him to come when he was about to leave on time. You know I just made these Coconut sweets yesterday, Shweta loves them and I wanted to send some to you. And guess who came at the right time? Don't worry, he won't be too late.'

'Okay, I won't say anything to him. That's what you wanted to hear, right?'

'Just a couple of minutes and he'll be right there before you know it. Achha Pooja, tell me one thing…'

'Go ahead'

'We both know how close these two are, don't they look cute together? I think they'd make a lovely couple, why don't we get them married?' she laughs.

Shivansh and Shweta can hear everything she is saying, she never leaves a chance to tease them so, they are nearly immune to what she says but today, it's a completely different story.

What just happened before they arrived makes their embarrassment tanks full, they cannot take more. Listening to her words makes their faces glow red. Shivansh looks away, half shy, half happy. Shweta asks her to stop doing that.

'Mumma, please!'

'I wish you could look at their faces,' they both laugh harder this time. 'Shivansh is such a sweetheart, I love him. You cannot imagine just how red his entire face is right now.'

'I know just how shy he is, but you won't believe he was a troublemaker when he was a kid, nobody does. I think our Shweta is perfect for him, let's get them married right after college.' Pooja is enjoying it just as much.

It goes like that over the phone for some time. Meanwhile, Shweta asked Kavya to bring the sweets for them but she, always not doing what's asked of her, doesn't. Shweta, with no other option, finds herself in the kitchen, placing plates over the slab. With everything ready, she just needs to get that jar from the cupboard but Shweta being not so tall cannot reach it. This means she's even more frustrated, she has to get a chair from another room. She takes a step back and her head bumps with something, she turns around to find Shivansh holding his chin in pain and laughing. He reaches for the jar before she can say anything. Their eyes meet, they haven't seen each other's faces since they left that place, he sees the slight redness under her eyes. *Maybe because she cried...* he thinks. She looks him in the eyes, *OMG! This is the first time I have ever been this close to him, except for that hug. That was so good, I felt millions of butterflies, I was flying, and he hugged me so tightly, more than I expected. It felt like he missed me, it was like he was carrying something really heavy and at that moment he was relieved of it. I can see his eyes, his nose, his jawline, his lips... I knew he looked good but seeing him up close is something else.*

'What are you doing?' she blurts. *Shit! Why did you say that, Shweta? Are you stupid? No, I need to say something else. How can I make it less bad? Ugh!*

'I was just trying to help you. I saw you trying to get that jar, and it was as clear as day that you couldn't.'

'At least say something, don't sneak up on me Mr Husband. It's not like you come here every day. Why do I have to do all the chores?' She laughs.

'C'mon yar!' They both laugh, and he grabs her hand. She takes a breath, he brings the jar and places it in her hand. They laugh harder.

Anjali looks at Shivansh with puppy eyes as he tastes the sweets, waiting for some compliments.

'Aunty, these are wonderful! When did you learn these?'

'Thank you, beta. Eat as much as you want, I made lots of it. Even packed some for you to eat later. At least try to let everyone else taste a piece.'

'Sure, thank you aunty!'

He gives Shweta a glance to convey that he is about to leave. She accompanies him to the door. They both go outside, where Anjali or Khushi can't listen to them talk. *Holding her hand would be too risky, what else can I do?* He leans towards her and says, 'Okay then, Mrs Wife, I think it is time to say *good night*'

Feeling a tingling sensation on her neck, makes her want him to get closer to her, *maybe it'd feel better if his lips touched my ears, just a little.*

'Hmm good night, Shivansh.' Trying her best to hide from him just how flustered she is right now but holding her neck and looking away from him gives everything away.

'Good night, take care.' He leaves. Looks back from the last turn after which he cannot see her house, she is still there, looking at him. She notices him looking at her and she waves her tiny hand. He waves back and continues to walk. Arriving at home, he thinks that his day is over but realises how wrong of him to think that as soon as Pooja opens the door.

'Welcome home, beta ji. What would you like to have?'

'Maa, please don't say it like that. You know what Anjali Aunty is like. Look she sent these for you, and I tasted them, these are great.' Opens the box and tries to change the topic.

'First, come in and get ready for dinner right away. We'll have some then.'

'Just five minutes.' Runs inside.

While having dinner, no one leaves a chance to tease Shivansh. Marriage, kids, grandkids everything is getting discussed. Being helpless,

Shivansh stops defending and takes all the jokes to the face since he just can't beat his family.

'So, Shivansh. When were you going to tell us about her?' Asks Vivek and fails to hold back his laugh.

'C'mon Papa!' he feels his face burning hot. *NO! I think my face is red they are going to mention that too. Calm down, Shivansh, calm down. It's going to be pretty hard but let's face it.*

'Don't you agree that she'll be a wonderful wife for him?' Pooja asks Vivek.

'Maa!' Shivansh begs her to stop.

'Couldn't agree more' says Vivek.

'I also like Shweta Didi! Will she be coming to live with us?' Says Tarun and everyone bursts into laughter, including Shivansh, Pooja is laughing so hard that she gets teary-eyed.

'Tarun shut up! Don't talk while you are eating. Maa, Papa, you are spoiling him, you are too lenient with him.'

All of Shivansh's efforts go in vain and Pooja and Vivek keep laughing out loud, holding their stomachs.

As always, Shivansh finishes his dinner after everyone else. He goes to bed, tired, hoping to get a good night's sleep after such a long day. Folds his arms behind his head and gets lost in his thoughts while staring at the ceiling. He is still trying to process that he confessed his feelings to Shweta, a second time, and how they are dating now, it feels different, better.

We didn't even get to discuss if we were telling anyone about us or not. He feels happy, close to satisfied, to have almost everything right this time, he has the love of his life, time to spend with her and gets to see her every day, and even better grades and skill in sports.

Fells asleep while thinking about her captivating, laugh he got to hear after waiting for so long, with a smile.

CHAPTER 10: DISTANCE MAKES THE HEART GROW FONDER

It's quite nice to wake up smiling every day and look forward to the rest of the day. The first thought that comes to his mind as soon as he wakes up with a smile. There's a pretty good reason behind that smile, he confessed his love yesterday. He jumps out of bed, and rushes through all the chores and breakfast, just to reach school before time.

Today, they look at each other differently, their gazes used to carry nervousness, anticipation, and restraint but right now their eyes are filled with contentment, they are no longer waiting, and they are no longer on hold or doubt. They are now sure of each other's feelings, they have been told what they wanted to for so long.

It's lunchtime and they both have come at the terrace to have lunch, together. Shweta is talking non-stop, not leaving a chance for him to speak something important he wants to tell her. Listening to her talk about how long she has been waiting for this moment, for him to tell her that he loves her, and how he has been completely oblivious and getting to hear those words from him was beyond a surprise. She is keeping up the pace of her blabbering and all he can do and wants to do is to look at her.

Lunch break is over, and Shivansh doesn't get a chance to speak, even a single word. *Girls...* he thinks. While going back to class, he asks her if they can meet at the usual place the next day. For two years now, they have been meeting at the same playground where they met for his match one day, to which she readily agrees before he can complete the question.

'You wanted to say something, right?'

'You are asking me that now? He says with a chuckle. 'I waited throughout the lunch to speak with you but kept going on and on about literally everything. And now that the break time's up, you are asking me what it was. Anyway, it's something important, I need some time and privacy to have a chat with you, alright?'

'Why didn't you say so sooner? Now all I want to hear is that. Can't you give me a hint? The suspense will kill me.'

'I told you earlier and I am telling you now, don't joke like that. I hate it.'

'Okay, sorry. It was just a joke. I won't do this again, but can't you tell me anything?'

'That's what you get for not listening to your boyfriend' he pulls her cheeks. She stops speaking and rolls her eyes.

'Awe, look at my tiny girlfriend getting all red' he laughs, she starts walking to the class without even looking back.

Shivansh takes a few quick steps and grabs her wrist, 'Wait Shweta, don't do this to me. And there's this other thing we need to talk about, are we going to tell anyone about us or what?'

'I don't know, everyone already thinks that we are dating. I think they will get shocked to find that we didn't, until now.'

'Yeah, right. So, we don't do anything. We'll behave like we've always been.'

'Yes…' she says, frees her hand and goes to her seat.

Sunday evening, Shivansh had a game in the morning, but rain made him drop his plans. Shweta waits for him at the slightly damp bench. She looks far at the empty swings swaying slowly with the wind, imagining herself and Shivansh on them. The sky wears gradients of grey from clouds, and the grass across the field looks vibrant green, rejuvenated by the recent shower. The breeze delivers the scent of wet soil to everyone around.

'Why do you always come so early?' he arrives from behind, and he notices the direction where Shweta is looking at. 'You want to go there?'

'And what do I say when you ask me the same thing again and again?'

'I didn't have anything to do anyway…'

'Exactly, and to answer your second question.' She gets up and gives him a tight hug. 'Yes, let's go and sit there for some time.'

He was not expecting this, he gets flustered and doesn't know what to say, getting hugged here of all places. He scans the surroundings and is relieved to know that there aren't many people around, thanks to the rain, and the few walking on the ground are too far to notice. Quickly hugs her back and asks to take a seat before someone gets an eye on them.

'Let's go then' he says and takes her hand, and they walk towards the swings.

'Where are we going today?' she asks, brimming with energy, smiling eye to eye.

'I don't have a particular place in mind today… Anywhere you want to go?'

'I won't mind if you show me another place you just discovered or haven't told me about yet.' Laughs softly but he cannot even smile. It is impossible not to notice, she knows something is wrong. She gently pulls his hand and places her other hand over his.

'What happened? It is rare to see you without that pretty smile of yours, you wanted to say something yesterday. Is it about that?' her voice conveyed how worried she was. Shivansh can look into her eyes and see that she is serious.

I have to tell her at some point, why not now then? He turns to her, putting her hands in his and says, 'Shweta, I am leaving in two months. Papa decided to leave his current job and get another one, they are offering better pay and a location close to our hometown. He is the only son so, no one is there to take care of my grandparents, they are getting older and need someone by their side.'

Everything falls mute, birds stop singing, trees and grass are moving soundlessly, and he can only hear his heart beating, it is the wait that is killing him, waiting for her to say something.

She starts looking back at the empty swings which are closer than earlier, imagining herself on one and another without Shivansh. The contrast between the beautiful day outside and the uneasy darkness inside them is too much to handle for such young hearts, perhaps this is close to a first heartbreak. First love comes with immense happiness, but the separation can cause great pain too. The thoughtlessness grows louder, not knowing what to do now is the helplessness they can't get out of.

Shivansh knew that the day had to come, and he kept reminding himself about the matter but today, he is not far from what Shweta is feeling. In this redo life of his, she is living for the first time, everything is new for her, she is clueless about every moment to come, unprepared unlike him, she only knows one thing, it is sadness that she is feeling right now.

He looks at her, but she is still looking at the swings.

'Don't be such a kid! We'll be in touch, in fact, I'll call you daily! Twice! They are sending me to a hostel so, I think can manage to call you pretty easily. Okay?' he forces a smile.

She still can't look into his eyes, her tears might drop and she's barely holding back, she starts to stare at their hands, wondering how long can they hold each other like this. He tries to speak again but his voice almost breaks, he stops and then gulps down a huge breath, 'Shweta please, don't make that face. We can do this, we'll have to just live apart for some time then we'll get the same college.'

Shweta looks at him with teary eyes and says something but her voice cracks, she loses control, and tears roll down her cheeks. He wipes them for her with his hand and takes her in his arms. She remains silent for a while then utters, 'Distance makes the heart grow fonder.' To be able to hear the same words from her after such a long time fills his heart with a mix of happiness and sorrow. He hugs her tighter.

They agree to keep their relationship intact, there is no other choice to begin with. They both know that they share something special that cannot just vanish if they live apart. Shivansh knew that everything would work out, after all, it did work last time. For Shweta this is something she has never experienced but so is this relationship so, she just decides to believe that they'll be fine, everything will work out no matter how far they are and how often they get to see each other, and they'll be alright if they just stick together.

As time passes, they start to meet more frequently and spend more time together. The closer the date when Shivansh leaves comes, the harder it gets to spend time without one another. On most of the dates, Shweta can't rein in her tears whenever they talk about him leaving and how they are going to manage that, Shivansh sometimes scolds her, and other times comforts her.

He hates seeing her sad, seeing her crying makes his heart tighter. Shivansh has already lived in a long-distance relationship with her, nonetheless, it is still hard for him, even though he had suffered from a heartbreak from breaking up with her, it is still hard for him, even though he's not a kid but an adult on the inside, it is still hard and painful for him, leaving her isn't easy no matter how many times he has already gone through the same or worse pain.

The day arrives sooner than they imagined. He has everything packed up, the cab is ready to leave, and all his friends are here to see him off except one, he cannot see Shweta. The cab driver honks and Vivek scolds everyone to get in the cab right now.

'Maa, please wait for some time, we are already leaving sooner than required for the train, aren't we?' pleads Shivansh.

Pooja instantly realises what's this about and asks Vivek to wait sometime. 15 minutes have passed but Shweta is not here, *she didn't even call...* he thinks. The cab starts to take the family to the railway station, his friends are waving their hands and running behind the car for a while, giving him a blast of a see-off. Ladies being ladies, are flooding tears, and men, well they are just standing and looking at them, some are even talking among themselves about the match they saw last night. *This is probably the last time I see these idiots,* he thinks as the cab leaves the society gate, he can no longer see those idiots.

They arrive at the station, everyone carries the bag assigned to them. Reaching at the platform, they find that the train is yet to arrive. The crowd is starting to get larger, continuous announcements are being broadcasted, stalls are selling fast foods, and sweepers are cleaning the floor. Tarun starts making a ruckus over some chips so, Pooja hands over some money to Shivansh to do something about him.

He takes the money and asks for two packets at the shop. Returning he sees a face that he cannot fail to recognise in a million faces, he is sure he just saw Shweta. But she is still trying to find him to give him a little surprise. He grabs the chips and runs towards her, she suddenly sees him coming to her. He stops a foot or two away from her, not knowing what to say or do, he cannot hug her here, saying anything in this noisy place wouldn't be the best idea either.

'Want some chips?'

'No...'

After a lengthy pause, Shivansh loses his patience and asks, 'Why didn't you come? You could've at least told me if you were going to come here, I was waiting for you. I thought I wouldn't see you today, for the last time. I mean we don't know how long it would take for us to see each other again.'

'I didn't want to cry in front of everyone...' she says with her eyes full.

'That's what you were worried about?' he laughs a little, 'I thought something serious came up, that's why you couldn't come. You should have told me.'

'You are about to leave me for god knows how long and you think there's nothing serious going on in my mind!'

'Alright, let's take a breath of fresh air. They are waiting for me I think we should go there first.'

He returns with chips and Shweta, gives Tarun his chips, Shweta greets Vivek and Pooja with her hands joined and gives Tarun a chocolate. Tarun is now on cloud nine, he will behave like a good boy for the next few hours, probably.

'Beta, why didn't you come to our house? All your friends were there too. Why come all the way here?' asks Pooja with concern.

'Aunty, the station is closer to my house so, I thought I should come here.'

'Okay, beta. You can have a little chat till the train arrives. Shivansh, go buy her something sweet.'

'Hanji mummy ji' he says with a smile and goes to a shop and gets his bag on the floor.

'What are you doing?'

'Wait…' he unzips it and pulls a small carry bag, taking her hand to give it to her.

'What's this?' she asks as she peeks inside.

'Some chocolates and a couple of letters I wrote to you. I started writing these as soon as it was confirmed that we would leave, I wrote the last one just yesterday. There are 13 letters, and I've marked them so, you read them in order, okay?'

'Hmm…'

'Hmm? That's it? I am leaving and we don't know when's the next time we might get a chance to meet.'

'What am I supposed to say? What do you expect me to say? You tell me that you are leaving a few days after telling me that you love me, one day I feel like I am at the top of the world and the next day I fall so hard that I don't know what to do. I know it's not your fault, it all happened so suddenly, I know it must be so hard for your grandparents to live all alone but these reasons and these circumstances don't mean that I cannot be sad.

It's not fair! Not to me, not to you, not to us! Do you have any idea how I'm going to live now? Even I don't know what I'm supposed to do without you. You know every day for the last two years was like waiting for you and then getting to meet you, that's it. Now that you'd be gone, I'll be all alone and I don't want that, I hate that. And don't you dare tell me that I have friends, I know I have friends, but I won't have you.' she loses all that's pent up inside her for more than six weeks.

Shivansh is stunned. He feels a weird mix of sorrow and contentment, *she really loves me,* he can sense the belonging he had always felt with her in his previous life and he knows by heart that he is going to miss her more than ever. *How am I gonna spend my days away from her?*

'You were holding back so much on your own, why didn't you tell me, Shweta? It must've felt so lonely, I am here for you. You don't need to hide anything from me.'

'I was not hiding anything from you, I just didn't want to talk about it. I wanted to spend time with you, happily, discussing this could only make us sad. And I was happy but for some days I couldn't get rid of these thoughts. Now that you are leaving, I thought I could tell you now but see it does nothing but make us sadder.'

'Awe! My princess is all grown up now.' He laughs and pinches her nose, 'At least it's off of your shoulders now.' It doesn't get easier or happier, but their beliefs get stronger that they can do this and everything will somehow, anyhow work in their favour.

The train has been here for about 5 minutes now, all three are on board and waiting for Shivansh to join them. It can depart anytime now but he has to give her a proper goodbye. He looks for something in his pockets, the train honks, he grabs her hand to give her a note and whispers in her ear, 'Shweta, I love you more than you know, and I'll miss you more than anything in this world. Please wait for me, we are going to meet soon.' Before she can say anything, the train takes its first step and Shivansh has to get on the train, he stops at the door and looks at her for one last time.

He can see her face getting red, tears rolling down her cheeks, she tries to wipe them off repeatedly, but they don't stop but she doesn't try to hide her face, she is only looking at him. She says something but it is impossible to hear but he can read her lips, she keeps saying, 'I love you, I love you, I love you…'

After a few seconds, they can no longer see each other, he goes to his parents, climbs up the upper birth and quietly rests on his back, no one asks him anything. At the station, Shweta stands still with a carry bag in one hand and a note in the other, still wiping her tears. She looks at the note, it is something Shivansh gave him just before leaving, it's much more than a piece of paper for her. She takes a deep breath to calm herself, something Shivansh nagged about all the time, and opens it.

> As I came across you,
>
> I sought more of you
>
>
> But now that I have you,
>
> I search for myself
>
> That you hold in your eyes.

This note isn't just a note for Shivansh either, he knows there's no need to write more than this, these five lines tell more than they appear at first. He believes that people fall short of the ideal their loved ones hold for them. Yet, therein lies the beauty of irony, the same people should strive tirelessly to embody the goodness and kindness their loved ones perceive. And he knows that he's no different.

CHAPTER 11: LIVING APART

'Like waiting for seven days wasn't hard enough to meet in peace!' Exclaims Shweta with a huge sigh.

'I know Shweta, it's hard but this is all we got. At least for now. If everything goes as per our plan, we can choose the same college, and this will be over in just two years.' Says Shivansh with realistic hope.

'So, we won't have a chance to see each other for two long years?'

'Maybe yes, maybe not…'

'What do you mean by that? Can we really meet? When? How?'

'I mean I can try visiting you, but I can't say for sure right now, I need to see how things work out here, I must have enough funds, and much more. Once I figure out all of this, then I can say for sure.'

'Yeah, you are right. It's been only three days since you moved to this hostel.'

'By the way, did you read any of my letters?'

'Yes, all of them!' she giggles.

'Seriously? Shweta, don't joke right now. I told you that you cannot read all of them, you must read them according to the date I've written on them.'

'I didn't, stupid! Not even one, happy? I'm trying to wait for the dates to arrive but I can't say for sure how long I can hold myself back.'

'You can do it, Shweta, it's not that hard for you. You are a good girl, you have already done this.'

'Shivansh, don't do that. It won't work.'

'What?'

'You know what!'

'Alright, I won't' he chuckles, 'So tell me how was your day?'

'Okay so first, I woke up early today....'

She begins to describe her day without missing a tiny detail, meaningful or meaningless.

He keeps listening to her, her voice going up and down with her mood, he can imagine the way she is making her face, how she is moving her hands, how she once in every few minutes twirls her hair with her fingers, how she rolls her eyes, how she smiles, everything. *I wish I could see her, right now.* No matter how they try, they cannot form the words and arrange them in a way that could express how much they miss each other.

Ever since he has come to this hostel, they can only manage some limited time to talk, they are hoping that they might have more time on Sundays and other holidays. They knew what was coming and they were prepared for it.

Listening to her for an hour isn't tiring for him, rather he feels like he'll have a pretty good sleep time. They decided that they wouldn't behave like a typical couple and waste hours on the phone so, they hung up after another half an hour. They need to study well to get selected in a good college. They want to be each other's strength, not holding each other back. They know that they must become happy, successful adults before they live together.

Slowly but surely, they are coming to terms with the distance and time difference between their schedules. From meeting on Sundays to staying on the phone for longer on Sundays, it surely isn't a change anyone enjoys.

Winters arrive faster than they were expecting, Shivansh tried his best, but it proved to be impossible to save enough money to be able to afford a trip to Shweta. *I never thought not having money could be this harsh. I am buying those shares as soon as I have an account of my own.* He has created a list of stocks that will give exponential returns all from his memory from his last life. This winter, they settle on having lengthier talk time on vacations.

'It's so cold!' he says, gulping down another sip of tea.

'Yeah, must be pretty cold there too. I saw the news, the temperature breaks another record in a decade.' They laugh a little.

'It's their usual.'

'One bad thing about living in the mountains is that you have to survive the winters' she indirectly tells her that she's the one struggling.

'Your mountains aren't that great, anyway.' He says with a smug face.

'So, any plans Shivansh? Don't tell me you've already completed your homework, why do you even have to finish it in the first week and how do you even manage that?'

'One question at a time please, I don't have any plans, I'll be lazing around here throughout the vacation, and I did complete my homework last night and now I can do whatever I want, no pressure.' He says with a smug face, Shweta can imagine him with the look.

'You are not going anywhere this time so, what are you planning to do with all the free time?'

'I'll talk to you…'

'I cannot talk to you all day, you know that right?'

'I'll talk to you when you are free, and I'll be thinking about you for the rest of the time. So, it's all figured out.'

'Seriously? This is what you want to do with all of your free time. By the way, I haven't even started my homework.'

'I know, I know. And I'm not asking you to rush your homework and talk to me all day, every day. But we can have some long conversations every once in a while, right? And don't you dare lie to me about your homework, you don't even take two weeks to complete? I think you have only a subject left, maybe two at most. Am I right or am I right?'

'Yes, you are Mr boyfriend. I'm left with only one. And I think I can manage more than once in a while long call, including today.'

'Great!'

The long call has to end at dinner time, which started right after lunch when both of their moms scream at them to put their phones down and join everybody for dinner. Most probably, they won't get their phone back after dinner. Shivansh has to rush but tells her something before hanging up.

'I have written something for you, not exactly for you. It's about my day but how can I write anything about my day without mentioning you, you are inseparable from my day, my life, me. Don't forget to check my text after dinner. I might not get my phone after dinner so, I think we'll get to talk tomorrow. Sweet dreams princess.'

'Okay, will do. Good night, take care.'

They go for dinner after disconnecting the phone call, at one end of the table Shivansh is getting an earful and on the other Shweta receives a nice lecture. Also, adding to the fire they are the slowest eater of their families but it doesn't go on forever, some topics change, moods change, they start laughing, talking about the day, *having dinner with everyone like this, every day, sure is a blessing,* he thinks.

After dinner they go to their moms and request to get their phones back, moms being moms, their hearts melt on hearing, 'Maa please, just the vacations. I promise I won't do this again' and they give them another last warning before giving back the phones. Shweta rushes to her room and looks at the text from Shivansh.

Shivansh

Nothing happened today,
Nothing out of the ordinary

Called some friends
Told some stories,
Listened to theirs and laughed

Spent some time doing chores
Talked to Mom and sang some songs

Sat with grandpa
Gained some grown-up wisdom

Now dinner's almost ready
Some are reading, some are scrolling
But only one is making
And I am talking to her
She's happy that I'm home

Some things did happen
Out of routine
But still nothing out of the ordinary

And yet, I feel a little less
I feel the moments that pass
Aren't good enough
The day went fine, in fact somewhat good
But somehow incomplete

I miss her,
No one saw this
As the day was fine

And I was smiling

I miss her voice,
Perfectly high pitched
And sweeter than honey
I miss her laugh,
Tickles my insides every time I hear

I miss her eyes,
Strangely, they seem something close to blackholes
Keep drawing me in
Away from everything else
And I know if I let myself lose, for once
I'll be lost in her eternity
Lucky I am since, she
doesn't look me in the eyes yet
else I'd have long gone

I miss her hands,
Those little things that whoever created
That I want to hold forever
I miss her touch,
The warmth it gives
The sound it delivers to my heart

And most of all
I miss the moment we sank into each other
The moment I had everything
Everything there was to have

And lost everything, every thought
As I witnessed her leaving
I felt a strange void in my chest
I grew fast but it began to hurt less
Either it doesn't hurt anymore
Or it has become a habit to bear

I do miss her every moment
That passes through me
But not like this, especially today
Don't know how or why
But I miss her
Even though it was not lonely
The day was good
I had chores to do
People to talk to

Wherever I was, she was somewhere in me
I seized all the chance
To look at her stills
But that couldn't last

As they call my name
I have to go
Leaving her stills behind, hidden

I miss her yet,
I go again with a smile…

I wish I could hug you right now! I have so much to say but I don't have the words like you do, I can just tell you that it is so relatable, I can actually feel the way you must have felt during the day, especially at the end. How can you even write such heart-touching and sweet lines? You are so creative, it makes me feel sometimes that you are doing so much for me, putting in so much effort and I am always at the receiving end, I don't do anything for you. I haven't done anything for you. I wish I was this creative, I wish I had something to cheer you up, I wish I could make you feel special like you do. All I know is that I want to hug you right now, I want to see your sparkling smile that radiates hope, your eye to smile that makes me feel butterflies in my stomach and I want to listen to those overconfident statements you make, they make me wonder how can you say such things that I cannot even imagine about.

The city you have left me with feels like a stranger to me now. The streets we used to roam around on, the places we visited, everything seems so unwelcoming without you. It's like I'm living in a different city.

> Shivansh, you make me happy. You make me feel special all the time, you make me feel loved. I know I don't have many options, but I can't wait to see you, come soon. I love you so much!

> Shweta, you have no idea what you have done for me. You don't have to do anything, okay? It's not like I feel I have to do all of these, they just happen. I don't even feel like I'm going out of my way, I feel so ecstatic whenever I do anything for you, though this may sound a little dramatic but believe me it's true. I do what I want to do not because I feel I'm obliged to do as your boyfriend. So, just trust me on this when I say that you have done a lot for me and I am the one who's lagging, and I am trying my best to catch up to you.

She wants to ask more about what he means by the last text, but she decides not to, she knows that he told her everything he wanted to. She calls him after reading everything he just texted, again and talks more, more about their love, love in general, and life. They dive into deep conversations that are bound to eat up their sleeping time.

'You know Shweta, I have this dream, like among other dreams. Ugh, like there are certain things in life I really want to do.'

'Yes, I'm getting what you mean. Just tell me what you want to say.' She assures her, which is all he needs, to tell her something that he has never told anyone about, except when he told her in his previous life.

'If I become capable enough, I want to adopt a child.' He says and waits for her to react. *Will she react like last time or...*

'I want to adopt a baby girl too when I become a responsible adult.' She says the same words with matching the energy when she said it to him for the first time.

He's struck by lightning! again! Just the way it happened last time. It is extremely difficult to believe that out of all the endless possibilities, they share the same dream, a dream that is not even a common one, like becoming a doctor or having a villa. Sharing a dream this rare seems like fate, even to a guy like him. It makes him question himself, is there a universal will at work that brought them together? Does the universe want them together or is it a mere coincidence? And just like last time, he now knows that he's ready to marry her and adopt a baby girl.

This time around he already knew about her dream but after changing the original timeline so much, he wanted to be sure, and it turned out that it was all worth it. His happiness knows no boundaries, his Shweta is becoming the Shweta he knew, the Shweta he loved, and the best part is he can see that happening right through his own eyes, unlike last time. Talking like this makes them feel so happy and at peace at the same time that they cannot help but wonder if it can be so much better if they are together.

'Talking about being together... I had a dream, about you.'

'Really?' she asks jumping out of her bed.

'I don't remember it in complete detail, but I'll tell you from what I can recall.'

'Just start with it already!'

'It was a nice morning, I know you are not a morning person but anyway, the clouds… they looked so pretty when they came down to touch the land, pretending to be fog. There were hills everywhere I could see so, the location must be where you are, and those hills were covered in green, topped with some bright shades of yellow, orange, red and blue. It must be spring, I think. Clouds were moving with the wind, covering everything in the water.

Then I saw you, wearing a cute light pink winter cap, a rosy sweater, a light blue pair of jeans and a pair of white sneakers. You were waiting for me, but you tried to act cool like it was no big deal. My heart literally jumped into my throat but seeing you so calm I tried my best to contain my excitement and behaved coolly, I think. You just gave me a simple smile, the way you usually do but I wanted to see you jumping here and there when you saw me after such a long time, I just smiled back and came closer to you.

I saw two bicycles parked there and you were with two other kids, they were younger than us, only by 2 or 3 years, but I didn't know them, maybe you did. They took one and left, instinctively I knew where they were going, and we were supposed to go there too. You hopped on the rear seat, and I started peddling. After some time there was no one around us, we were flying through the clouds, I didn't know where I was going.

Unexpectedly, two arms covered my neck from behind and those tiny arms were yours. I loved the way it felt, I think I can still remember how it felt. Weird right? It was a dream yet, I can remember how it felt but it indeed felt realistic.

I was caught off guard so I blurted out, "What are you doing?" but you were not even listening to me. You just kept shouting, "Yes! Yes! Yes! Finally!!" again and again.

Seriously, it was so realistic, I could feel your weight over my shoulders when you hugged me, your warmth, the loss of balance on the cycle when you suddenly hugged me so tightly, screaming in my ears the smell of your recently washed sweater. I tried to tell you to stop so many times, but you didn't listen once, we could have fallen, you know, but you kept saying the same thing at the top of your voice. Sadly, then I woke up.' He says, wanting to have something more to say.

'That doesn't sound like me at all! So much excitement, such loud expressions! But it was a nice dream, cute. It feels so good to be a girl who comes to her boyfriend's dreams. Am I that pretty?' she chuckles.

'Yes, you are! You are the prettiest and cutest!' he says honestly.

'Now I don't know what to say...' she says awkwardly and waits for him to say something beautiful to make that awkwardness vanish.

'Shivansh? Shivansh!' she raises her voice, 'Did you fall asleep? Shivansh...?'

'No, I'm listening' he says after snapping out from his half-asleep state.

'No, you are not! You were sleeping.' She giggles a little.

'I was not sleeping Shweta, please continue what you were saying. We are off topic now.'

'Really? Then tell me what I was telling you?'

'C'mon Shweta, you don't have to corner me like that. At times like these, you pretend to agree with what your boyfriend says even if you know it's not true. You should have told me what you already did from the start.'

'Alright, is that what I am supposed to do…'

'C'mon now, tell me again, please princess…' he tries to go for her weak spot.

'It won't work Shivansh and it's not like I'm angry or something, but I think you should get some sleep. I know you are tired, you had a long day doing all the chores and look at the time, you should go to bed now.' She says but he doesn't reply.

'Shivansh? Did you… Are you sleeping? Hello?'

'No, I was just thinking…'

'Shut up! You were sleeping, I can tell by your voice.' She says in her cute angry tone.

'I'm not lying, I didn't sleep this time.'

'You are going again with this, tell me what I just said. And what or whom were you even thinking about?' she's pretty annoyed now.

'Whom?' he laughs, 'My little Pokémon is jealous. You were telling me to sleep because I had so much to do today and how late it was.

And I was thinking how nice it is to get to talk to you in the middle of the night, I am here in my room, away from the cold, you over there in your room, it must be even colder for you.'

Bam! He's struck with an idea. He continues to say before Shweta can say something, 'Wait, Shweta! I just got this great idea. You are not sleepy, are you? Can you wait for me for five minutes? I'll be right back, okay?'

'I have no idea what you are talking about but alright, I'll wait.'

'Great!' he says with a broad smile and jumps out of his bed to get a pen and a notebook. He has got the idea, all he has to do now is to play with words and arrange them in a way that can give that idea life. Sundry words come to him, but he ignores most of them and handpicks the ones hiding in the tough spots. His idea breathes life but as he looks at the time, he finds that 23 minutes have passed, he asked for only five. Nevertheless, he types what he has just written and taps the send button.

> Inside a room, isolated from the freezing winter I feel bliss upon hearing your words
>
> Shall I ever seek again and find you
> I can only wait for a dream to come true

Since he didn't text back in five minutes, then in ten minutes still no text, she started to read her book. Lost in her book, she fails to notice a notification popping on her phone screen. Thinking that he didn't text back, she gets annoyed and picks up her phone only to see his text that came 17 minutes back. She quickly unlocked it and saw his text. She reads it, then she reads it again and before she can text him to ask if he's awake, she gets a call from him.

'You wrote this? Like yourself?' she says with some surprise.

'Yes...' he replies, confused, 'This is what came to me when we were talking.'

'Shivansh you were already quite good, but you've improved, this one was really good. It was so simple yet so touching, you expressed so much by writing so little. That's something.'

'So, you liked it right?'

'Liked it? I loved it stupid! One on hand you write something as good as this and on the other, you are so clueless.'

'Well, I didn't get the chance, but I wrote some more lines a while back when I was waiting for you the whole day but since you had exams you slept early, we couldn't even talk much, for several days at that. I told you not to study overnight but you did and then you got sick after your last exam, that's when I wrote this one.'

'I know, I know but we do have plenty of time these days, don't we? Like we used to have. And don't make me wait so much, just send me what you wrote, please.'

'This is nice, you can make me wait for days and I can't even make you wait for a couple of minutes. Also, I wasn't even going to make you wait but now I like the idea.'

'C'mon Shivansh!'

'Alright.' He laughs, 'I'm sending you that let me find it first, you get your headphones meanwhile, I don't think you can switch the call to the speaker.'

'Yes, give me a second.' She plugs in her earphones and looks at her phone, waiting for another text.

> Unbearable silence and lonely night
> Cold winds keep me awake
>
> I look for the moon
> It whispers back your name
>
> Gives me warmth
> And the night is not lonely and cold

'Shivansh, tell me one thing, were you outside that night?' she asks with concern.

'What do you mean?'

'You know exactly what I mean!'

'Yes, I know... you told me about your fever and after dinner, I had nothing to do. I tried studying but couldn't focus. Then I tried watching anime, even some movies but nothing worked, I felt a little out of breath. Earlier, it was easier to wait for your exams to finish because I knew we could talk as much as we wanted after the exams but when you fell ill, I was expecting to have a long conversation with you but it ended so abruptly. I had so much to talk about, so much to tell you from what I'd stored for days. Then I went outside to get some fresh air.'

'Get some fresh air? Are you out of your mind? You went outside your house in the middle of the night during peak winters.' She shouts a little.

'Let me finish first,' he laughs and continues, 'So, I went to the roof and yes it indeed was cold, the winds were so strong and cold, but it was so beautiful, the sky was completely clear and the moon shined so brightly. It was amazing. The moon looked somewhat as beautiful as you, not winning though, and that's when I came up with these lines. In fact, I didn't even think much about it, I just wrote what happened. Now, I have a question for you, how did you figure that out, that I was outside that night? Don't tell me the second line gave it away.' He laughs again.

'To some extent yes it did but the way you wrote it, or you usually write, I can feel what you must have felt when you were writing, maybe it's the way I read what you write, maybe it is the way you write, maybe it happens to everyone or maybe it happens only to me.'

'If I am a good writer then it can happen to everyone, else you are a good lover and only you get what I felt while writing.'

'Stop with the buttering. Why'd you go outside when it was so cold? You could've gotten cold too!'

'What's wrong with that, you got sick, I get sick, not bad.' He chuckles a little while liking the idea.

'No, that's a stupid idea. You get cold so easily, take better care of your health, stupid!'

'Yes, mam! But I still have so much butter left, what should I do with mam?" he laughs, and she joins him, they both laugh for a moment.

'Okay, one last chance for today, no more cheesy lines.'

'Shweta, have you heard people blabbering about getting the moon for their lover, some even compare their lover's face with the moon, but I would say that you are like a half-moon.'

As Shivansh had anticipated, she asks him instantly, 'Why half?' with a slightly frustrated tone.'

'Because my dear princess full moon always shrinks down. While the half-moon always grows...' for some time no one says anything, he waits for her response, but she has no idea what to say.

Then he suddenly remembers something, before he can say something Shweta says, 'How do you even come up with these things?'

'Shweta, can you wait for a while? I just remembered something, it won't take long.'

'Something urgent?' she asks reading the pace of his voice.

'You'll see…'

He remembers an event from his past life when he was scrolling randomly on his phone, he saw a video in which a couple found out that the phase of the moon on their respective birthdays was waning gibbous and waxing crescent, and when put together they formed a full moon.

He was deeply touched by this so, he wanted to check the same for himself and Shweta. He quickly typed Shweta's birth date on one tab and his own on the other tab, and he was blown away by the results. He had a waning gibbous on his birthday and she had a half-moon on her birthday, they don't combine to form a full moon, but she had a half-moon on her birthday, the way he called her a half-moon. This much was more than enough.

He searches for the same now and takes a screenshot, he sends it to her showing her date of birth and a photo showing the phase of the moon on that day i.e. a half-moon.

'Told you, you are a half-moon.'

'God! Seriously, how do you even come up with such things?' she asks in a mix of shock and awe.

CHAPTER 12: THINGS PEOPLE DO FOR LOVE

'Things people do for love…' Shivansh replies to the question she asked twice.

Shweta is speechless, he's always saying something, something to make her lose all her words so, she just says, 'Umm hmm…'

'It is always amusing to make you speechless, the way you say "Umm hmm" when you don't have anything to say is pure bliss' he chuckles.

'Shut up, stupid! Why do you even do all of this? You know that I am low maintenance, but you still do so much.'

'Because I love you, what else? And like I told you I don't see this as work or something I have to do. I like doing stuff like this for you, that feeling when I think how you'd smile at something I did, really gets my heart racing and when you do smile, it all gets worthwhile.'

'Ugh! Not again! I don't know what to say to that.'

'You don't have to, I know you…' he waits for her to say something, but she remains quiet. 'Well, if you still don't know what to say then I'll give you something to speak. Give a brief explanation about how handsome your boyfriend is.' He controls his laugh.

'Woah! Or kuchh?'

'Nope, I know you won't even say a word after your classic "Or kuchh". On a serious note, have you read my letters yet?'

'Yes, all of them except one, the one with my birthdate on it, can't believe you thought this far ahead.'

'You have no idea how far I have thought…'

'But do I really need to wait that long?'

'Yes, otherwise it'll be a complete disaster!'

'I know right? Had I read even one before the date mentioned, it would have gone so wrong. All your dates were so intentional. But I didn't, right? So, do not worry.'

'You better stick to it!'

'Yep, your letters are safe with me. Tell me one thing, when are your vacations ending again?'

'I need to get back on the 8th of January, classes start on the 9th.'

'Shivansh, it's been months since the last time we saw each other, can't you find a way so I can see you? You always figure something out, please tell me there's a way. I want to see you...'

'I know Shweta, so do I. I wish I had wings, then I could just come flying to you whenever I wanted. I tried everything but there are some circumstances this time, I'm low on money and it's really hard to leave home before the vacations are over, they know when I need to get back. I think I might pull this off on my next vacation. Can I ask you to wait a little longer for me?'

'That line... "I wish I had wings..." Was that from one of your pieces?'

'No, I just said that without thinking.'

'It was a nice line, it made me feel butterflies in my stomach, like so many other times.'

'Alright, I'll see if I can make something out of it. But you didn't answer...'

'Of course, I'd wait for you. It's not like I have other options but I'm ready to wait for you even longer. And I think it is better the way it is, some things are not supposed to be confined in pages but cherished in memories.'

'Woah! You are getting a hang of it, aren't you?'

'*Tera asar hai...*' she sings a line from the song "*Kaun Mera"* by the artist *Papon.*

'Stop it! What happened to you? You are in the zone today!' They both laugh hard for a while.

'I don't know I just went with the flow, I think luck played a big role because that is it from my side, seems like my zone has faded away.'

'You were amazing! You know that? You are amazing!'

'Yes, that I am.' She chuckles.

'Okay then, I think we should get some sleep before the sun rises or else we might get some real scolding this time.'

'See ya.'

The lengthy phone call ends with successfully dodging the reprimand from their mothers. They don't usually call for so long, nor do they call each other every day, mostly on alternate days. Today, like many other unplanned days, they had so much to talk about that neither of them wanted to hang up, and in the end, they weren't even sure if they were happy to get to talk for so long or sad because they had so much left.

The day Shweta has been waiting for months has finally arrived, she can open the last letter at midnight, but she has to wait till the time he tells her to. It has only become harder each day for her to hold herself back and today it is the hardest of all. She's struggling to wait for the night to arrive when it's only just the morning, the clock seems a little too much slower than usual, especially slower than the time she calls him. She keeps asking him if she can have a peek, but he doesn't budge.

'Shweta, you have been waiting for months then why are you so hung up on opening it now? I'm telling you if you open it before I say so, then it'll get messed up. I don't want that to happen but if you do then do it. If you prefer reading a letter written by me than talking to me then go ahead.'

'Why are you getting so grumpy? You know how hard it is for me to wait for something like this. And I know I've been waiting for so long but the less I have to wait, the harder it gets to wait.'

'I know Shweta... just don't think about it. Let's keep talking and eventually, we'll get to the point when I will ask you to read it. Simple.'

'Like I can actually do that.'

'Just kidding, we'll get there don't worry. You can do it, my little princess.'

Shivansh has a plan, he is sitting on a bus to Nainital. He'll be there by evening. He tried his best to meet her during his last vacation or rather that's what he told her. She has no idea what he's going to do.

A perfect surprise, he thinks. The excitement to meet her after all this time has kept him awake since last night and she's been awake for the same length since she can hardly suppress her urge to read what he wrote about a year ago only to be read today. It is after lunch when he starts to feel his eyes going against his will, but he can sleep since he is hours away from the city where Shweta lives.

This is not a present for her, in a way, it's for me. He had planned a surprise visit for her birthday, but little did he know that they would break up before that.

He starts to think about old times, his eyes slowly get heavier. It is getting harder to stay awake. Steadily, his consciousness fades and his thoughts get intermingled with his dream, he starts to dream about the day they met for the first time after they started dating previously. Like most of his dreams, he cannot tell it apart from reality and smiles in his sleep.

He had started his journey at 10 p.m., and the moment he got on the bus he started talking to her. It was half past one, he would be there with her in the morning yet, they were talking like there was no tomorrow. Maybe it was she who wanted to somewhat digest the fact that they would see each other the very next day.

'I wish your mom were there, I truly wanted to meet her.' He said honestly.

'*Or kuchh?*' she replied the way she used to whenever he asked for something impossible for her.

'Seriously Shweta, your mom's so cool!'

'Really? It sounds like you know her better than I do.'

'C'mon yar, remember the last conversation you had with your mom? You only told her about my trip to Nainital and she, without even you asking, readily told you that you could meet me. I was literally blown away when you told me that. I could never expect something like that.'

'Yes, I could tell by your reaction.' She laughed, 'You had asked me so many times if I could come to see you, but I couldn't say "Yes", not without her knowing. And the way you kept asking me if I was joking about that, it was so fun.'

'And you kept saying, "Do you seriously think that I can joke about something like this?" and that made me convinced that you were not kidding at all.' They laughed for a while. He unintentionally woke the lady sleeping next to his seat, but she must have been so tired that she didn't say anything to him and went back to sleep, maybe she didn't even realise that the boy on the next seat disturbed her deep sleep.

'Shhh! I think we woke her... I think she went back to sleep, we are good now. Wait, I'm good now, she can't say anything to you, can she?'

'Yeah, whatever. And Mr Shivansh, you didn't tell me about that "her" sitting next to you.'

'Yes, there's a woman on the seat beside mine. Are you really jealous about that? I've been talking to you since the moment I got on, I didn't even talk to her and honestly, I just looked at her when she was trying to get her luggage up there because I didn't want to get hit in the head by her bag and after that I didn't even look at her.'

'Yeah, yeah, whatever but you didn't tell me a woman is sitting right next to you.'

'C'mon Shweta, stop acting like this. I know you are not mad or jealous.'

They continued to talk for another hour and decided to sleep, neither of them wanted to feel sleepy on their first date or worse, sleep when the other was in the middle of saying something.

Shivansh got off the bus at seven in the morning, as expected. Booked a cab as soon as possible and ordered a plate of *Aloo ke Parathe* at the reception, before he even asked for the key.

Changed from his comfy clothes to something more suitable for a date and sent a mirror selfie to some of his friends to ask for a quick review. He decided to go with a plain blue shirt under his off-white jacket with a pair of black denim and white sneakers. He had bought the jeans two days back only when Akash begged him to buy one and look decent enough for a date. Shivansh being clueless about fashion nuances, didn't know what to wear. So, he took his friend's advice despite thinking that getting dressed wasn't even necessary. "It's not all about looks." As he used to say. On receiving his photo, Akash felt a sense of relief to see his friend not looking too casual. He instantly replied, *"Bro, you are all set! Now go and have a nice date."*

With all the reviews he received, he concluded that he was date-ready. He finished his breakfast and left the room. On his way, he kept checking if he had taken everything with him that he would need for his date. Reached the place where she asked him to come before her, way before her, and texted her. He could feel his blood rushing to his cheeks, he could feel them getting warmed up, his heart beating faster the more he thought about seeing her after all these years, as her boyfriend. His mind was running all over the place, but he stood still, waiting for her.

His phone rang, he carefully took it out, trying not to accidentally answer it before he was mentally prepared but it was not from Shweta, but from his friends which he found out to be a group call when he picked it up. Some nonsensical talk from his friends was all it took to make him feel at ease. Even though he was bombarded with questions, he was calm.

'How's the date going?'

'Does she look the way she looked in her photos?'

'What are you guys doing right now?'

'How's she? What was her reaction?'

'Where are you two going? What's the plan?'

'What did you get for her?'

'Can we talk to her? We just want to greet her, we'll say, "Bhabhi ji Namaste!" Please let us talk to her, just once.'

No one in the group could tell who was saying what, they all started laughing. When there was enough silence, Shivansh told them that she was not there yet. He didn't say so, but he was thankful to all of them, it was because of them that he could then think straight again.

'Guys! She's here! Bye!' he said the moment he caught her first glance, he couldn't even see her face but he knew the woman he was seeing coming to him was Shweta.

She was coming down from a slopy-curvy road and he could see nothing except her. Her loose hair made waves with the slow wind, it looked like they were made of gold in the sunlight, and she looked like an angel. He wasn't even sure if he was breathing but he didn't care, he didn't care about anything else. Her eyes made the sun and moon shy, she was wearing a mask covering half of her face. He then noticed something, he was not expecting that, but she did get her eyebrows done.

Did she... Should I ask her? She might feel good that I noticed, maybe she would feel embarrassed. Ugh! What should I do?? Honestly, I don't like this idea of getting eyebrows trimmed in perfect shape, they look weird... And worse I think she overdid it a bit. What if she asks me about it? I don't think I would be able to answer her honestly. What if I blurt out something like, "Maybe, you shouldn't have done it..." And I if try to lie then she would just know that the instant I open my mouth. What should I do? Think Shivansh think! His brain wouldn't stop! Soon he noticed something else, something he should have noticed a while back if he were in his right mind, she was coming towards her.

His brain stepped up a gear, it started throwing more thoughts at him. *Shivansh, leave the eyebrows and look at her. She's coming! You know exactly what you are supposed to do right? You've thought about it, you are all prepared. If we are talking about being introverted then you are nothing in front of her, you know that she, most probably, will not even shake hands with you. All your simulations showed you just one possible event, she will wave her hand from a metre or two away and so will you, then you two will head where you are supposed to go. She's almost here... anytime now, Shivansh, get ready, don't embarrass yourself with a weird wave but how do you even wave your hand exactly, there's no rule or technique, is there? If there was, then you would have practiced that too but does something like this even require practicing? Shut up! She's right in front of you! I didn't expect her to get this close. Look, she's lifting her hand, she's going for a handshake. That's a bit unexpected but you can do it! I know you didn't think but it's just a handshake, you are a handshaker, don't think much just go for a nice and firm handshake, and it'll be alright.*

'Hi!' she said, looking at her eyes he knew she was smiling but her mask was hiding it.

'Hey!' he replied, and his brain kicked in again. *Dude! Her hands! They are so small! Like a child's. How can hands be so soft and warm? I know you want to hold it longer, but it'll be awkward, to see she's pulling her hand back. Go ahead and kiss her hand! No! Don't you think it'll be too much? It will be too much for her, it'll be too much for you! Drop the idea, you can't do it. You can't do anything.*

Shivansh was then ready to follow her lead, she had told him about a place where they'd go on the first date. His brain kept rumbling, he was waiting for her to turn and start walking but he noticed that she was not moving at all.

She raised both of her hands and pushed all her weight on him as she was standing on higher ground. She was light. The scent of her hair was mind-bending and that's how he found out that he was breathing indeed. His constantly blabbering brain was overloaded with everything that was going on, and it stopped, he could no longer hear anything going on in his head. Her hair kept covering his eyes, but he didn't mind that at all, he loved the way their cheeks touched each other's softly. Her tiny arms were wrapped around him, and his hands subconsciously moved and hugged her back. There was something different, something that felt nice, happening while they were hugging, he was moving in a cute side-to-side motion along with her. He didn't want to do anything else but just be there, at peace.

On the road, he beautifully makes her walk on the outer edge of the road without letting her know what he was doing but little did he know, she saw through him easily. Shweta was not acting the way he had imagined, she was a lot more talkative than she was on the phone, she kept telling him about random stuff, but he couldn't hear a thing. He just nodded to everything she said as if he was listening to her attentively, he was too busy only looking at her.

He saw Shweta for the first time after they had started dating, the first time after eight years when they were classmates, he had seen countless photos of her, but he had no idea what it was that was so different about that day that made him so enchanted by her. He loved the way she pointed at things with her miniature fingers, it was indisputably one of the cutest things about her.

By the time they reached the bus stand, all he had heard from her was "Hi" and after that, he was completely oblivious of what she was going on about. They took a bus to go where she was taking him, he could go anywhere with her. Only two seats were available for them so, they rushed and sat side by side on the last row.

The moment the bus started moving, he realised that he was in a tough spot. The driver was quite the racer as he drove through turns without slowing down, making the idle passengers fall left and right. Shweta was on his left, the last thing he wanted her to think about him was him taking advantage of the situation and falling on her each time a turn came around. He grabbed the pole next to him with all his might and forced his body to stay still despite the sharp turns.

Glad that I worked on my core! He thought and laughed inside. But whenever a left turn came around, he couldn't help but be thankful to the driver and the roads that made Shweta fall on him. Sometimes, she just grabbed his shoulder, the other times, her hair came in front of his face, and some turns made her head touch his cheek, he was really glad to take the last row seats.

The "*comfy*" ride ended in half an hour of bliss for him, they got back to walking. He was still recovering from his *loss of hearing* and gradually, it all started to make sense what she was saying. She frequently switched between telling something about herself and her two besties. Sometimes, she spoke about her family. He kept nodding and opened his mouth after a long break to say, 'Are we here?'

'Yes, this is the place.' She smiled, as she pointed at the board with *Eco Cave Park* written on it.

They joined the queue to get the tickets, but he noticed that she was tired of all the walking, so he asked her to take a seat while he bought them for her. He came back within five minutes, and they had a real conversation as Shivansh was also speaking every once in a while. Rested enough, she thought it was time to look around the park. They began walking and Shivansh saw a place with almost no people around, they could see the hills and the city from there, it was the perfect place to spend some time.

They sat side by side, Shweta again on his left. Again, she was the one speaking and he kept looking at her.

'Your hands are so big, mine are so small. It's quite hard in touch typing.' She said after a while jumping from one topic to another.

'Yeah, sure but I think they are cute.'

'That, they are. Let me have a look,' she asked for his hand, he placed his hand over hers, palm up.

'I didn't think the difference would be so huge.' She placed her hand on top of his, palm downward. They continued to play with each other's hands, looking at them from both sides, comparing the lines on them, the veins, the texture, the nails everything. The silence was comfortable.

It broke off when her phone rang, she chaotically pulled her hand and searched for her phone in her handbag. It was from her friend, to ask her about the date. She kept talking to her for a while, telling her not to disturb them. Shivansh was waiting for her to end the call, he took his phone out and clicked a picture of her. She snaps and looks at him as if saying *What are you doing?* But he didn't listen and took another one. He was waiting because he had been hiding something he had brought for her, tucked halfway in his jeans from behind and the rest was hidden under his jacket. Each time he adjusted it while walking, he hoped that she wouldn't hear the noise, she didn't, not even once.

The phone call ended, and he pulled the present out for her, felt the immense satisfaction of seeing the glow on her face.

'Can I open it?' she asked with a cheerful face.

'Yes, it's all yours but I need to ask you something important first.'

'What?'

'Are you going to remove that mask of yours?'

'Oh this... I don't know, I like this trend. I don't have to show my face to people, they don't know what kind of expressions I'm making. Even if this Corona situation goes away completely, I'm keeping this on.'

'So, I'm not going to see your face today? Sad, I came all the way here just to see you.'

'Okay...' she removed her mask and wiped her face, 'I just forgot to remove it, I don't want to wear this when I'm with you. You won't believe I even wear masks at home.' She chuckled.

Shivansh was again in awe. *Just how many times is she going to make me feel like this,* he thought.

'Can I open it now...?' she pointed at the present.

'Yes, yes, please go ahead.'

She started to peel off the wrapping delicately, trying her best not to rip the cover as if she didn't want to hurt it. Her thumbs and fingers were covered in band-aids from all the cooking she had been doing since she had started living without her parents. She told him that she was so clumsy that she couldn't cut an apple without getting hurt.

He felt strange, something strange in his gut, to see her gentle fingers covered in band-aids, he wanted to take a closer look at them, kiss them but he kept staring at her hands as she tried to open the present. The band-aids at the tips of her nails kept getting in the way of peeling off the tape on the wrap. He asked her if he could help her, but she wanted to open it herself, stubborn as she was.

She finally managed to peel off two main pieces of tape and after that, it wasn't hard to go with the rest. She could tell that there were two things in the packet, yet she was surprised to look at them. The first thing was a colouring book, Shivansh remembered when she told him about her visit to a stationary shop with Khushi one day.

There she said, 'Look at these colouring books,' but she replied unexpectedly, 'Are you a kid that you want to buy a colouring book?' and to top it off the old lady at the shop heard her and started laughing at her. She got embarrassed beyond measure and left the shop in an instant. Shivansh laughed a lot when he heard about this even when he promised not to, but he remembered that she wanted to get a colouring book.

Her second gift was a journal. Shivansh knew that she used to write journals on certain occasions so, he spent hours looking for a perfect one and got it for her.

'This is such a thoughtful gift, you remembered about the colouring book too. I'll send photos after colouring each page.'

'That's a nice idea. I didn't think of that.' He spoke.

She began to put them aside, he continued, 'Wait, open that again.'

'The colouring book? But I just did, it's beautiful.'

'No, it's not about that just open it again.'

She again flipped the pages, slowly this time, and found a page. She opened it only to find out that it was the same page she asked him to bring, he had written a poem for her and sent her a photo of it, but she wanted the original handwritten copy, so he did bring it for her. She was pleased to receive it but she didn't let her face tell him everything.

After talking for a while Shweta asked him to walk on the other side of the park, they both wanted to have a walk in peace but unlike his friends, hers kept calling her. He wanted to grab her by the waist or put his hand over her shoulder while they walked but he didn't want to give her a shock while she was on the phone. He held back for so long and finally said, 'Tell them that you are absolutely fine, and you'll talk to them after this as much as they want to.' Thinking the same thing for quite a while, she tried to end the phone within a few seconds.

'Let's take a snap!' she said right after she hung up the phone and took a photo of their shadows on the road, in front of them.

After that, they experienced some silence for a couple of seconds, he tried to hold her hand, but before his hand could reach hers, they were next to a bench, and she went ahead and sat, asking him to sit with her as well. He sat again calculating the perfect distance to be maintained with her, neither too far nor too close to make her uncomfortable.

They continued their talk for a while, she told him about the calls she had been receiving ever since she left her house, who called, asked what, and told her what to do. Unlike Shivansh, she had tonnes of things on her including a water bottle. After talking so much for such a long time she felt the need to drink some water, so she offered some to him as well. He tried not to overthink about sharing a water bottle.

Soon they got back to walking again, to the other side of the park. He saw a perfect place to click some photos, the place had flowers, hills far behind in the background and correct lighting.

'Shweta, didn't I tell you that, unlike others, I'd take some awesome photos of you? I think we can start here, this is the spot, go over there and give me a broad smile and I'll handle the rest.'

'Or kuchh?' She used to say this whenever she didn't want to do something.

'What? Is something wrong?'

'Don't you know me…?'

'C'mon Shweta, it's nothing! Just give me five seconds and it'll be done. You won't get the chance to say that no one takes good photos of you.'

'No… I don't like posing and stuff, maybe next time. Okay?'

'Okay…' he said in a low tone, 'wait, I've something else for you. I forgot to give it to you earlier.'

'You have more? Just how many things did you get for me?'

He was walking on her right, she was holding her bag and the gift in her right hand so, she drew her left hand to take what he was handing.

'No, give me the other hand,' he said.

She then grabbed everything in her left hand and tried to get it with her right hand, he was hiding something in his hand. To her surprise, he wasn't hiding anything but acting like he was, without saying anything he grabbed her hand. She moved her eyes from his hand to his face, but he started looking away from her to hide his embarrassment.

They took two steps like that when she tried to loosen her hand, he became worried if what he did was too much for her, but she wasn't trying to untie their hand instead, she wanted to change the way they were holding hands. She slipped her fingers between his and said, 'That's better...'

'Yes, it is...' he said, finding it hard not to show his happiness on his face. Realising again how small and soft her hands were, he felt the need to click a picture of their hands, in contrast to his expectation, Shweta readily agreed.

He again took her hand in his when they were sitting on a bench, and she got a call. He started to play with it, drawing imaginary lines, looking at her hands from all sides, gently tracing her palm with his fingers. *Wait, is that really... Can I really feel her pulse? I'm not even trying, and if I listen carefully then I think I can hear her heartbeat. What is going on? Is that how she feels when I touch her hand? Does she really love me that much? The body and the heart cannot lie, can they? What is this I can hear it so clearly, her elevated heartbeat, am I the one causing it? Even her face is red, is this from the winds or is it me? She looks kinda... nervous... Is this love?* Her phone call ended.

'I could literally hear, not just feel but hear, your heartbeat!'

She pulled her hand in an instant, he could see the bashfulness on her face. He knew what it meant. They stayed quiet for a while.

'So, you are not going to let me take photos of you?' he broke the silence.

'No, I won't,' she said in a cute way that hinted otherwise.

After that he kept taking her photos randomly without even asking her, sometimes they turned out pretty good and sometimes she realised before he could take one and hid her face.

They left the park before sunset as it would get really cold really fast after that. She had a journal and a colouring book with her, and he had many photos of her. Both were happy until they saw the road filled with monkeys. On trees, on the road, on the side rails, they were everywhere.

Shweta was terrified of monkeys, so she grabbed his arm tightly. He reached over the moon and thanked the monkeys for their pleasant presence. He kept assuring her that they wouldn't harm her and that if anything goes wrong, he will take care of it.

'Just don't look them in the eyes. They feel judged...' He cautioned with a hint of joke but bad timing. She couldn't laugh but it certainly did calm her nerves somewhat. Slowly, they started to see more shops, and roads with people more than the monkeys, this meant Shweta could let go of his hand, neither of them wanted that but she was too shy to keep holding his arm in that crowd.

'Now you are getting all shy? What about earlier?'

'There I was way more scared than I was embarrassed…'

They reached the place where they got off the bus to walk up to the park surprisingly, it was almost empty. They took a seat in the third row, she wanted the window seat and he wanted to see her happy. When the bus reached the last stop, Shweta remembered that they didn't even get one photo of them together so, she proposed to take a selfie. Shivansh being the worst guy to ask for a selfie, took his phone a captured a not-so-great-looking click. Shweta, thinking that she didn't look great in the picture, asked him to delete the photo but he didn't. They began to walk to the place where they had met in the morning.

On the way, Kavya joined them. Shivansh greeted her warmly and only spoke a few words, being the introverted guy he was. She complimented his choice of shoes and the trio kept walking. He wanted to walk closer to Shweta and put his hand in the back pocket of her jeans or at least on her waist but was conscious about Kavya.

The sun was about to light the other side of the world, leaving this side in the hands of the moon. They reached the place from where they had to go their separate ways, at least for today.

Kavya went ahead leaving them alone for a while waited for Shweta near the intersection. Again, something happened that was beyond his capability to anticipate, she hugged him the way she did in the morning to say goodnight and he felt like he was melting again, this time less shocked though.

Shweta waved at him from a distance before she went ahead to catch up to Kavya. He was left with no choice but to head back to his room, thinking about the date he just had.

On day two, Shivansh got up late, all the travelling and late-night calls were quite draining and was rushing to get ready to leave on time. Ordered the breakfast, shaving, brushing, getting the water perfectly heated, checking the outfit for day two again, everything all at once.

Stuck between all of these chores he still managed to get a mirror selfie to get feedback from his friends, again. The phone started ringing somewhere in the pile of clothes, he threw some clothes here and there to find it and saw her name on the screen.

'Hello,' he said and before he could say anything further Shweta said, 'How long are you going to take *Dulhe raja*?'

'I'm ready, okay. Are you already there?' he tried to hide his feelings, that feeling when you feel good inside about something but have to act in denial to everyone else.

'No, but I'll reach there in five. Just tell me when you leave.'

'Alright then, I'll text you when I'm there.'

'Sure'

Shivansh was ready to leave, he checked again if he had everything with him and locked the door. The "day 2" present couldn't fit inside his pocket or anywhere on his body so, he carried it in his hand, which felt weird. He decided not to call her when he reached but to get a handbag for it first. At the gift shop, he saw various items that he could get to add some extra charm to the present. He bought a tiny teddy bear that could fit in the small handbag he got with the present. But he was still missing something, so he went outside and asked for the flower shop. Heading for the shop, he called Shweta to check if she was coming from the same direction and luckily, she wasn't. He rushed to the shop, bought a rose, and came back running to the place where they were supposed to meet. He looked for a place where he could hide, he didn't want her to see him first.

He texted her to give him a ring when she reached the place. On reaching, she did what she was told to and asked for his location, he told her to keep walking, and he would find her. He opened the camera on his phone and started recording a video, the next moment she was in the frame, he called her name, and she found out the place he was coming from, and began to walk towards him.

'Hey! See, same-same,' she pointed at the handbag she was carrying when noticed one in his hand, hers had a different design on it. Shivansh offered her the present and then the rose, she brought the rose closer to smell it and asked, 'Should I carry it now?' pointing at the bag.

'Yeah, sure. It's for you…'

'Alright, let's go.'

They started walking, he realised that they hadn't hugged. *Why didn't we hug today? Was that a one-time thing? No, because she hugged me again. Then why not today? Are we not doing that again? I don't know how long will it take to see her again, I want another hug! Ugh!* Several thoughts crowded his mind. He decided to be optimistic and gave himself a reason for not hugging i.e. because of the gifts, both were carrying something with themselves, it was hard to hug comfortably or maybe it was because more people were there than last day.

He kept following her, listening to her. She had told him that the view around the temple was just epic, and she had asked Khushi to join them, she would also take some photos of them. She started panting after walking some steps to the temple they were going to visit. The path was harsh, the elevation was too much for Shweta. Shivansh was also short on breath, but he kept talking in a way that hinted that he was completely fine, he even offered to carry her on his back but, Shweta being Shweta, she kept refusing. He saw a shed on their way and before he could suggest something she asked him to rest there for a while.

Shivansh asked her if she wanted to unbox today's present, she opened the carry bag to see a cute little teddy bear sitting on a box, and she smiled. She took out the box after the teddy and started peeling the wrap neatly again, he started recording her secretly or else she would stop him.

'Didn't get your reaction last time.' He spoke.

'I don't have "reactions." You know my mom was so impressed by you when I told her that you gave me a colouring book. She was like, "Such a thoughtful gift, don't go empty-handed next day!"' They both laughed a little.

'Really? I knew it, your mom is cool.'

She was opening the present when he started to notice her all-black outfit, it really suited her. He then remembered what she was wearing previously, black bell bottoms and a light caramel sweater, he felt stupid for noticing something so obvious so late, maybe he could only look at her face and nothing else.

'The packaging was done by me, it should be easy to unbox.' He claimed.

'Just how many boxes did you pack?' she exclaimed at the fact. As the wraps peeled off, she saw a black box and she instantly said, 'Is this a watch?'

He was caught off guard to listen to her accurate guess, 'Yeah…'

A mint green watch with gold accents, she smiled and tucked her hair behind her ear, Shivansh saw this in slow motion. She removed the watch she was wearing to try the one she just received.

'How does it look?'

'Perfect, just the way I imagined it would and I asked too late…'

'What…?'

'You know I asked you earlier if you have a watch and you said that you bought one a while back, about a month or two. The thing is I had already bought it by then. There's something quite nice that happens with me, sometimes when I see something be it a shirt or jacket or watch, a face pops up in my head, telling me upon whom that thing would look great and when I saw this watch, I saw you wearing it. I wasn't even planning to buy anything for you but that watch just came to me.'

The glitter on the carry bag started to spread all over her and she was covered in it. 'I think I'll be shining the whole day…' she laughed softly. *You are always shining…* he thought.

They kept talking, sitting comfortably under the shed. For a moment they even forgot that they were heading somewhere. They went back to that strenuous road to reach a children's park where Khushi was supposed to join them.

'Is there where you shot that video of you and Khushi swinging?' he asked as they took a bench.

'No, that was a different park.'

'Okay, and why are sitting under direct sunlight, it's too intense.'

'One, I love sitting in sunlight and that's how I survive winters here. Two, you'll feel cold if you sit in the shade.

'Okay…' he said and removed his jacket and hung it on one side of the bench.

They again dove into conversations, Shweta talked more, and Shivansh nodded more. She got another phone call and started talking. He felt the urge to guide a lock of her hair behind her ear and tried to do so, Shweta acted calm when he reached for it but he couldn't do it perfectly. She laughed a little, and he tried again, still not perfect but better than earlier. This happened because he was too shy to touch her face so, he tried to tuck her without touching her which proved to be impossible. She smiled and did it for him and hung up the phone.

Somehow, when she was talking from one topic to another, she suddenly said, 'You know some people are so unprivileged, I feel sad for them. And I feel so grateful for what I have, I'm so lucky.'

He was dumbfounded, she was actually sad when she talked about the struggles of some random person, her voice couldn't lie, and her sympathy for others was boundless. *I can't even feel this sad if someone I knew gets hurt and she's actually sad for someone she doesn't even know. I think she can ride the Flying Nimbus from Dragon Ball, only someone who is pure of heart can ride that cloud if I remember correctly, I know I can't ride it.* He thought.

'Care for one pic? Just one!' he asked with great hope.

'I told you I don't like taking photos of me...'

'Then what about a selfie? I have a good idea.'

'Okay... let's see your idea.'

He asked her to turn around while sitting and look at his phone over the bench backrest, he softly said, 'May I...' before putting his hand over her shoulder and clicking two photos with smiles on both of their faces. It came out great.

Shweta noticed Khushi coming from afar while talking to him and went to talk to her. Then the three headed to the temple. Shweta was obviously overjoyed to see her best friend, Khushi was unique in her way. She resonated with the aura of someone who doesn't know about the workings of the world, she needed care and attention, and her energy was equivalent to that of a lazy cat. The moment she joined them, all of Shweta's attention went to her, he kept watching Shweta acting in a way he had never seen before. He wasn't even jealous about it, he was curious to see this new side of her.

They reached the temple, and Shweta and Khushi prayed for a brief moment while Shivansh waited for them. They walked further and arrived at the location with a scenery to behold. It was the golden hour, and Shweta didn't want to miss that opportunity. She asked Khushi to take pictures of them together and she did her job with excellence. They got some of the best photos together.

After talking and laughing a lot, it was time to head for the next spot. Walking down the slope was less exhausting and it started getting colder, cold enough to make him wear his jacket again. They talked about random stuff, he was expecting that Khushi would also be a dog person just like Shweta, he was the only cat person in the group.

Simz café, they arrived there with nothing in mind, it was another nice place to take some photos. They were not dinner-hungry, but they could grab a few bites.

'You've been here, you should know the best table and the best dish they make.' He said the obvious.

'Twice at most, if not only once,' she said, hinting that she had no idea about the table or food.

Shivansh took the lead and chose a seat near the window on the first floor, they could see the street from there. One thing they noticed that they should have noticed earlier was that the table was next to the kitchen, and the staff kept going in and out which was a bit irritating.

He wanted to sit facing Shweta, but she wanted to sit next to him and Khushi on the other side, he had no choice.

'We can click some more photos this way,' Shweta said.

'Hmm good enough. Let's order something first and then we can get some photos clicked while we wait.'

Khushi took some more impressive photos, and some short videos too. Waiting made them hungrier, the pizza and noodles were a bit too spicy for him, and he kept drinking water to deal with that.

They saw a man taking his husky on a walk, it was Shweta's dream to someday own a husky with a golden retriever so, it wasn't unexpected to see her overexcited.

'Look at that cute husky! He's so small!' she wanted to go and pet the husky.

Shivansh forgot that he was a cat lover and said, 'Yes he is adorable, I think I want one.'

'Sadly, they can only live in cold places, you can't have one. Or you can move here...' said Shweta in a teasing tone.

'That's the sad part, otherwise, I'd get one as soon as I get the feeling that I can handle someone other than me, and what about golden retrievers? Where do they live?'

'I think they can live almost everywhere. When are you planning to get one?'

'Let's see...'

With their stomachs full, they realised that it was almost time to leave. The sun being not so considerate, began to set on time. Shivansh would leave the city in a couple of hours, they wouldn't see each other again for quite a long time. Sadly, the bus stand was quite far so, Shweta couldn't see him off since her parents told her to go back home before it got dark, it would begin to get cold with time.

Shweta whispered something to Khushi before she left, and the two of them began to walk in silence for quite a while.

'When's your bus?'

'At 10 so, in about 4 hours...'

'Sorry, I can't come...'

'It's alright, I know your family is worried about you and it is quite far from your house.

Even I'd say that you should go home instead of seeing me off.' He said wondering about what she was telling Khushi, but he soon realised what it was about when he saw her coming back.

'I asked her to get me something...' Shweta said.

'I figured!'

Khushi gave Shweta a chocolate and left, for real this time. She put it in the carry bag she brought for him and handed over the bag to him. *She was carrying the bag the whole day and now she's giving it to me,* he thought.

'What's in it?' he asked, knowing about it.

'Well, you can look for yourself. I didn't wrap it up so, you can find out easily. And you do know what's inside, the chocolate she just gave me, that novel, *The Notebook,* you gifted me and yes now it's your turn to read it, and the oversized T-shirt I told you about. That's about it, nothing special.'

'You don't have a clue how special this is!' he said with a spark in his eyes.

They kept walking down the slope yet, as they moved forward their steps became slower. Neither of them wanted to leave so, they kept delaying the inevitable. Unlike the previous day, they are not going back to the same place they met in the morning but halfway to her house where her cousin would come and pick her up. Shivansh would go back from there, two days were enough to know this much about the streets.

The unwanted time finally arrived, and they reached the place. She could even see her cousin waiting for her from afar. She called him to tell him that she would take a few minutes to come.

Shweta looks Shivansh, in the eyes, after spending two whole days with him. He opened his mouth to say something but before he could, she hugged him with all her strength, Shivansh held her tight for the little time they were left with. He could feel that the hug wasn't a "I'm happy to see you" hug but one that echoed "Don't go". Her eyes said the same thing when he saw them getting full of tears.

"Shweta, don't get emo now!' he said trying to cheer her up, the last thing he wanted was her tears, 'Let me make a memorable moment now…' He gently moved his fingers through her hair and pressed his lips on her forehead with his eyes closed.

Her filled-up eyes didn't dry in an instant but neither did they shed a tear, her cheeks turned red, and she gave him a smile that bewitched his heart. They let each other go but their hands did not, they were standing apart and their hands were slowly loosening their hold, and their fingers felt the last touch. Shweta started walking backwards, Shivansh didn't move, he couldn't move, their eyes refused to look anywhere else. She finally turned around and continued to walk. Just before she could no longer see him, she turned around again and waved at him, he waved back, standing at the same place. She took a left turn with her cousin, and he could no longer see her.

He wakes up with tears rolling down his cheeks, he feels a lump in his throat. He snaps back to reality and wipes his face, drinks some water and realises that he was dreaming. It was a nice dream, but he never saw her again after that day. He looks around if someone sees him, but no one does, he looks at his phone, 09:30 pm. *About an hour left...* he thinks.

10:40 pm, he books a cab from the bus stand.

11:55 pm, Shweta is holding the last letter Shivansh gave her and asked her to wait for her birthday.

Midnight, she ignores all her phone calls and messages, opens the envelope and finds out that unlike other letters so far, this one is shorter, way shorter to be called a letter, it is a note saying...

> Look outside the window, now!

She cannot believe what's written on this piece of paper, she holds her breath and jumps out of her blanket, it's cold. Hesitantly walks up to her window to see outside, she can see someone standing there, in the snow, waving both of his hands towards her. She instantly realises that he is that stupid boy who loves her like no one else, he is Shivansh.

She dials his number, 'Happy birthday princess!' he shouts so loud that she hears him through the window.

'Shhh! You'll wake everyone here, please no more shouting'

'I know, I know, just couldn't hold back. I really wanted to do this once in my life. So, Happy birthday princess! Are you free tonight?'

'I literally have no words, I could never imagine you would show up like this. Aren't you cold?'

'Nope, It's quite warm outside. Why don't you join me?'

'What do you mean "join you"? I cannot come outside.'

'C'mon Shweta, it's the middle of the night, you'll be back before anyone even wakes up. And Tanya can handle if something goes out of plan.'

'No Shivansh, I really cannot come.'

'Shweta, it's your birthday and I have prepared something for you. Can't you take this one chance for me? Please…?'

'Ugh! Why'd you have to do this? Wait, I'll be there in five and if I don't come then assume that either Mom or Dad woke up, okay?'

'Yes, ma'am.'

She puts on as many layers of clothing as she possibly can and sneaks out of the house, successfully. Tanya was up, she closed the main door from the inside and locked their shared room. It is freezing outside, he wraps his hand over her shoulder and takes her to the cab waiting for them. They close the door, and she hugs him tightly, 'If you had a cab booked then why did you go outside? Stupid!'

'Anything for you, dumbo!'

The cab drops them off and he takes her to his room, blindfolded. He removes the cloth from her eyes, all the lights are turned off and the room is filled with candles, she then looks down to see a beautiful cake in front of her. He hands her the knife, and she blows all the candles in one breath. She cuts it and they both give each other a bite. He asks her to wait and gets a card and a box from the almirah.

'What's this?' she asks and opens the card.

'Your birthday present, genius!'

'I know that much, I meant what's inside?' she begins to read the card.

SHE WHISPERED...

It's early morning
Sun's a little shy
All red, peeking through the horizon
Soft light sneaks through the curtains
Kissing the pearl-white walls
Faintly lighting the cold room

I am sleeping
It's later than my usual
But I want to sleep more

Then she comes
Wearing my shirt, not fully buttoned
Climbs on me, laughing softly
Holds my face in her tiny hands
Leans over me, her hair hiding my face
Kisses me and whispers to me
I kiss her back and look at her
I'm not sure what she said but I liked it
She goes louder
Wake up! And wake me up!

I struggle to open my eyes
Turn to my left, and there she is
Hiding under the blanket
Leaving nothing for my eyes
I pull her blanket to see her
She resists, and then reveals her face
I kiss her eyes and pull her closer
I ask her to wake up
She caresses my cheek
I kiss her hand and put my hand over hers
She smiles and whispers to me
I'm not sure what she said but I liked it

She looks back at him.

'I had this dream a while back and I wrote it like this. So, tell me Shweta, what did you whisper to me?'

'Stop being so irresistibly cute!' she says and picks the box to open but Shivansh takes her hand and pulls her closer to stand next to him.

'Let's save it for later. For now, I have something to ask you, care to dance?'

'Yes!' she nods repeatedly.

He plays "*Tum se hi*" from the movie "*Jab We Met*" on a Bluetooth speaker. Their bodies start to move slowly with the track. Remember from all the tutorials he went through, he places his one hand on her back and holds her hand in the other with elegance. She is surprised that he can do that, she did see him perform in group dance, but she has never seen him like this before. She places her hand on his shoulder and moves along his steps.

They move closer and hold each other in their arms and move even slower, she can feel his heartbeat, it's calm as if he's home, he loves the way her head is touching his chest, he rests his chin on her head. They keep moving slowly, eyes closed.

I think it's about time I drop her back, it would be a disaster if anyone finds out about this, and I can meet her in the evening or for lunch maybe. He moves his hands and gently holds her shoulder to create a short distance between them, looks her in the eyes and says, 'So, how was your birthday present?'

Shweta cannot say a word, she grabs his shirt and pulls him back. Their faces are next to each other's, and their breaths are heavy and out of rhythm, she holds his face and goes on her toes to reach his lips.

Shivansh is about to kiss her, for the first time, in all of his timelines. Their breaths come in sync and they move closer. Suddenly, he feels like his heart is drowning, he gently stops her and moves back. She could tell that he was about to kiss her, but something happened that stopped him.

'What happened Shivansh? Are you okay?' she asks, terrified.

'Shweta, there's something I need to tell you. I don't think I can live with myself and with you if I don't.'

'Shivansh, no need to hurry. Let's take it slow, I'm here for you.' She takes him to the bed and gets him a glass of water.

He gulps down the whole glass in an instant and says, 'Sorry to ruin your birthday. I wanted it to be perfect, I wanted to make you feel special and I wanted to tell you how much I love you.'

'I know Shivansh, you don't have anything to apologize, okay? It is because of you that I feel like I'm at the top of the world. You always make me feel special. Things like this can happen at any time and to anyone, you cannot blame yourself. Now take some rest, I'm here until you feel alright.'

'No, I need to tell you first. There cannot be a *right time* for something like this.'

She takes his hands in hers and says, 'Only if you feel better...' her eyes speak that he can tell her anything.

He wants to tell her everything, everything about his past life, how he died and woke up back in time as a teen, and what he went through.

He tries to speak but as soon as he opens his mouth, it feels strange. His throat is burning, and pain in his heart increases as if someone is crushing it, this time it doesn't feel like guilt but actual pain. He cannot say a word no matter how hard he tries, he grows pale with each passing second, he tries to breathe harder but cannot feel the air filling his lungs. He loses consciousness.

Shweta keeps screaming, 'What happened Shivansh? Don't worry, I'm calling an ambulance. I won't let anything happen to you, stay with me.'

He struggles to open his eyes, it's too bright. He feels a sharp pain in the back of his head. He can hear continuous "beep" sounds near him, the room he is in is white. *Am I in a hospital? What happened to me? Did Shweta bring me here?* As his eyes adjust to the brightness, he starts to see some familiar faces surrounding him.

Wow! Such a memorable birthday present for Shweta, I don't think she's ever going to forget this. And how long have I been here for, to make all these fools come here to see me? He moves his head to find Shweta but then realises something is strange, there are faces that he does recognise but he has yet to meet them. *Why is Shivi here?*

And Loki, Suhel, Tannu, everyone! Why are they here? I haven't met them yet, the time has not come to meet them so, why are they here? How do they know me?

He keeps looking around and finds that Shweta is not there. He begins to recall everything that happened to justify what's in front of his eyes. Bang! A thought comes to his mind which aligns that has happened so far. *Am I... back in my original timeline?* He thinks. He does not want to accept it, he looks for Shweta and then sees a calendar hanging on the wall, with "2026" written over it in bold. He cannot deny this anymore. *But I fell... How am I alright? I don't think anyone can survive a fall from that height.*

Everyone is looking at him, but no one says anything, they are waiting for him to come to his senses.

'Don't tell me you lost all your memories asshole!' Loki breaks the silence.

'What happened Shivi?' he says in a low tone.

'Restaurant staff found you unconscious on the floor. You've been out for three days! Your parents called me asking about you, I told them you were just too busy so, you couldn't manage to call them. Now Shivansh, tell me what exactly were you doing there?' asks Shivi in a stern voice.

Shivansh realises what must have happened, some pieces still don't fit together but he'll think about that later. *I cannot believe I lived for over three years just to get back to this! Was all of that a dream or am I back to this timeline? But whatever the case, this is where I am right now, gotta handle this first.* He decides to get out of this scene first.

'I was just trying to get a perfect sunrise from up there but when I asked the manager the day before, he didn't listen to me. And you know me, I had to do it especially since I wasn't allowed to. Then that morning I did see it and when I turned back to get back… I think I slipped or something, don't remember what happened. By the pain, I can tell I must have hit my head.'

There is silence again in the room, then everyone bursts out laughing.

'That's so you, bro!' says Suhel while laughing.

Loki, the most unpredictable character in his life, leans towards him and whispers, 'Bro, I have something to tell you, remember that long-ass letter that you wrote a while back?'

'No, you didn't!' Shivansh shouts with his eyes out.

'Oh, I did!' Loki laughs harder.

Everyone starts laughing again, they are relieved to know that it wasn't what they feared it was. Shivansh is really worried about what Loki has done and what is going to happen now. Without warning, everyone stands up and starts to leave the room, the last one to leave is Loki. He turns around at the door and says, 'You might want some privacy...' and shuts the door.

She's been standing behind the cubicle curtain in the room, listening to every word Shivansh and his friends were saying. She walks past it and stands next to him.

Shivansh is now looking at Shweta, she looks the same when he saw her last time. But her face is red, her beautiful eyes are red. Tears are gushing down her eyes, her lips shivering. She stands in front of him, squeezing a bunch of crumpled papers in her hands, the pages that contain his feelings, the pages he wrote with his heart, the pages that together can be called a letter, the only letter he didn't send her, Shivansh's last letter to Shweta.

CHAPTER 13: THE LAST LETTER

To the part of my soul,

I'm baffled by everything that's going on. I wonder what is easier, to fall in love or to fall out of it. And if falling out of love is even possible, I wonder if it'll ever happen to me. I love you more than I ever imagined I was capable of, and I felt you loved me too. Believe me, it took a hell lot of time and courage to believe you did. It is hard to stop thinking about you, to stop missing you every fleeting moment, every breath reminds me of you. You made me believe in this so-called "love" and showed me the breathing magic in its evident perpetual existence.

I know I pushed you away and I understand that you don't want to get back, but couldn't you stop me from going? Couldn't you ask me one more time if, I was sure? If, I was, okay? Couldn't you call me?

Didn't you love me?

Was it so easy to let me go? Was that how much I mattered to you?

I know saying all this is useless now so, I stopped a long time back. I didn't get all my answers but if you are happy without me then that's all that matters. Last time we talked, when I told you to block me from everywhere. I don't know if you did but thinking that you did, I was able to hold myself back from contacting you. This "last" letter that I am writing is the only thing I have written to you ever since that day.

I'm not sure how it happened but I was always the "facts and numbers" guy, I never liked poems as a matter of fact, I never even understood poems, and maybe I never tried. So, what made me write all those lines for you? I think we both know the only reasonable answer is you like you always have been. You are worth writing poems about, you are worth singing songs about, you are worth writing books about. If a guy like me could do this much for you. If a professional artist ever tried to create something for you, that could've made the world go crazy. Sadly, I wasn't that great, but I tried to be great, for you.

I know that you've made up your mind and you are not the one to ever change your decision, but I don't know why I keep expecting your call whenever my phone rings.

What happened, happened. I have to come to terms with it. I broke up with you to make sure that you don't get dragged into my mess, I know I wasn't right or just. And the worst thing was that I wasn't strong enough to uphold my resolve and stay away from you. You are a strong girl, you helped me to stay on my word and I cannot thank you enough for that. But you've become an integral part of me, and it'll take time to build myself and my dreams up from scratch, without you, if that ever happens. I doubt that there will be a night when I look up in the sky and see a half-moon and not think about you.

You used to call me your sun, you said that I bring warmth and light into your world. I know I was always cheerful and happy and smiling but it wasn't that way. It was you who made me smile all the time, you were the sun in my life, it was your light that shined through me, a lifeless rock that people see as the moon.

Many days after we stopped talking, something happened and I couldn't stop coughing for days. When I went to a doctor and told my symptoms, he asked me to get checked for tuberculosis and the first thing that came to my mind wasn't the fear of death but the fear of not seeing you at my deathbed or worse you coming back to me to find that I'm no longer here. Running through tests, one day my ECG was being monitored, being the romantic, I wanted to try something, I wanted to test if something like this could happen in real life. I started thinking about you and I don't know what to make of it but my pulse jumped over 140, while I was in bed! It was, in its own way, quite funny.

Totally unrelated but a weird thought came to me that day when I got to see a patient with memory loss, what if I lose all my memories? And how would my heart react if I saw you then? Will there be something similar or will there be nothing? Will my eyes shed tears for you or will they fall in love with you, again but for the first time?

One day, I started writing something, when we were together, but I couldn't finish it and after we broke up, it just became easier to complete it.

REMEMBER ME

I hope that this is not the end
But somewhere I know, it might be
We'll go our separate ways
We'll live our own lives
But remember me

It might annoy you
It might cause you pain
But remember me

Remember the boy
Who was mad for you
Remember the ordinary boy
Whom you made special, just by being with him
Remember the uninspired boy
Who was inspired by you and wrote
Remember the "play it safe" boy
Who bet everything for you

> Remember that narcissist idiot
> Who became selfless for you
>
> Remember me
> the way I was with you
>
> But if my memories become a burden
> And thinking of me makes you sad
> Forget me...

Maybe you have forgotten about me, maybe you remember me, maybe you remember me just as much you remember any other person that came into your life for a brief time, maybe you still love me but I know you are strong and stubborn, you'll not come back to me even if you wish to. Sometimes, I do think what if you come back? What if you come back when it's too late? I think it'll never be too late for the love I have for you will not fade but it will be too late someday for us to be together. You don't have much time, please come if you are going to come, it's not too late yet. But then again, I know you won't come back, I know you will not say that you love me.

I don't know if I wrote this letter to you who once loved me or to me who never stopped loving you.

I can keep writing this forever but I know I have to stop at some point. I have this last secret to tell you, I felt happy whenever you called me "stupid", weird I know but it always felt like I was "your" stupid boy. I wrote this utterly long letter just to rot in my cupboard hoping that it finds its way to you by some conspiracy of the universe. Why? Isn't it obvious at this point? Because I am stupid!

-Ever yours

Milton Keynes UK
Ingram Content Group UK Ltd.
UKHW030639191124
451300UK00006B/78